A RULE OF THREE

Book Three of The Knight in the

Panther Skin Trilogy

An accurate English prose adaptation of Shota Rustaveli's epic 12th century Georgian poem.

H. J. BUELL

ANA GABUNIA

https://hjbuell.com

COPYRIGHT AND PRINTING

ISBN-13: 978-1-7379516-4-3 – eBook
ISBN-13: 978-1-7379516-6-7 – Paperback
ISBN-13: 978-1-7379516-8-1 – Hardcover

First Printing, August 10, 2023

For Ana, who sacrificed more for Georgia than most people will ever know. May you forever have the courage and strength for unexpected journeys.

ACKNOWLEDGEMENTS

ARTWORK
Irakli Kakhadze, Cover Artwork
Dasha Vainstein, Layout and Design

CONTENT EDITORS
Michael Arizola, Tyron Eugene Byrd Jr.,
Dane Muckler, Ph.D., Rose Marie (Peggy) Parris,
Abbi Seid

DEVELOPMENTAL EDITORS
Zobaid Alam, Luka Bandzeladze,
Lucie Isabelle Sylvaine Dubail, Diana Kakhidze,
Benjamin Kastin, Alexander Edward Loughead,
Loïg Seigneur, Marek Suliga,
Khatia Turmanidze, Edward Wilson

MUSIC AND AUDIOBOOK
David (Dato) Toradze – https://toradze.ge

SPECIAL ACKNOWLEDGEMENTS
Darina, Veronica, Angelina & Max,
Desert Knights of America MC, AS from Reddit,
Josiah Keola Blair, Julie Cheung, Ali Farhad Howaida,
David Jakobia, Rishi Lakhani, John Jeys, Virgil Jones III,
Tina Mamulashvili, Patrick Naughter, Lasha Pataraia,
The Rat, Sea Dog, Rezo Tchelidze, Tom Vainstein,
Marjorie Wardrop, and Chef Gustavo from
https://www.blankslateband.com

CONSUMED BY THE SUN

H. J. Buell

Empty are the hours
Between love and loss
Where wilting flowers
Measure time and cost

Is forever an
unwritten poem
Or an open hand
When walking alone

Down forgotten streets
And roads not taken
It's there we will meet
Hearts unforsaken

Weave silk for your gown
Then reach to the sky
With stars as your crown
And heroes by your side

For you are the one
Who makes this love true
Consumed by the sun
I belong to you

... you know who you are.

PREFACE

A Rule of Three is the third and final book of an adventure few people outside of Georgia have ever heard of. It's the culmination of an adventure spanning almost ten years and most of the known world. More, this book is a faithful adaptation of the original Knight in the Panther Skin, composed by Shota Rustaveli in 12th century Georgia.

Although little is known about Shota, the poem's prologue indicates it was written to praise the first female ruler of Georgia - Tamar Mepe (King Tamar). Some believe Shota was in love with her, as his writings allude to this. But, like all great works, the original is not without controversy or debate.

To this day, his writing is a pillar of Georgian culture. It stands alone as the most significant literary accomplishment of Georgia. The original poem is written in Rustavelian Quatrains, consisting of four sixteen syllable rhyming lines. In total, the poem comprises 1,662 of these, totaling 6,648 lines. Each year in Georgia, there are people who recite the entirety of these verses from memory at annual events.

We've done our best to accurately capture the spirit and meaning of the story. However, cultural, and linguistic barriers limit the ability of anyone to fully express the true beauty of this text in anything other than its original Georgian form. However, what you read in this book is the most honest and accurate adaptation of Shota's poem as an English literary novel.

For additional resources, comments, and information about the country and traditions, please visit our website.

https://hjbuell.com

TABLE OF CONTENTS

INTRODUCTION –

PART ONE: THE CITY OF KUTAISI

I left the theater with an uncertain step, no longer sure of the ground I was walking on or where to place my feet. Though I couldn't say specifically what caused the disorientation I was experiencing, I felt myself poised on the edge of some great discovery. Everything around me was surreal.

It was as though I stared too long into the looking glass and got caught in the reflection of a time long since passed. Old streets and buildings seemed to echo forgotten moments and memories. Each of them tempted the writer in me. Still, I was committed to seeing the end of my journey before chasing any other old Georgian legends.

However, I could no longer refer to what was happening as my journey. The experience had taken on a life of its own. I was sure my meeting with the man in the wine bar from Kvareli was no ordinary encounter. Such a person was impossible, yet the story he told had substance.

It was a real thing, no matter how surreal my experiences were. And the theater I just left was also real. But I could not explain the old man or how the dance in Kutaisi pulled me out of time and place. Nor could I explain why, but I was going to make my way back there tomorrow evening.

There were more things left for me to learn in this ancient city of artists. I had no doubts about this. But I couldn't just go home. Too much of my mind and spirit remained unsettled. So, I would busy myself discovering more of Kutaisi's sights and smells in the space between tomorrow and tonight.

Unsure of which direction to head in, I made my way toward the river. My steps took me past a quiet moonlit park. Statues peeked out at me from beneath old trees as I walked by. Each was tucked away with their secret histories and stories of everything and everyone who ever walked past. Fountains sang quiet melodies, an accompaniment to the shy couples pretending to be busy with anything other than new love.

Whatever I saw tugged at the corners of my eyes. It pulled my attention to ghosts and shadows of histories I was painfully unaware of. History and humanity had grown and fed from one another for thousands of years in this place. So much happened here. The sum of my life wasn't even a whisper. My existence could be counted in the space between a leaf falling and touching the ground.

It's not to say I was nothing. But instead to point out how life-changing the experience was for me. I felt like a lone man standing on the shore of a beach in the last seconds before a tsunami of time engulfed him. In the context of Kutaisi's vast history, my presence added less weight than a feather. My passing to or from here seemed almost meaningless.

But what defines meaning? Who decides the value of a

person? Is it their contribution to society? Do we measure their worth from the monuments built when they're dead, or is it something less tangible? Was the who of a person was more important than anything they could create, or was what they created a result of who they were?

I didn't know, but as my thoughts wandered, so did my feet. Soon the sound of the Rioni river rushing over rocks beckoned me forward, and I was treated to the sight of a unique and lovely bridge. Bits were made of glass, showing the waters and white stones glistening below my feet.

The metal had been cut out in many places with sentences written in beautiful Georgian script. Each sentence was from a different writer, all about Kutaisi. Beneath the bridge, a series of lights were artfully placed to shine through the letters and illuminate the artwork.

Curious to see more, I kept walking. Soon I lost myself in a maze of old buildings and older streets. Most of the night, I wandered like this, content to immerse myself in the history around me. Besides, the surety of a river to guide me home meant I couldn't possibly get lost. But I didn't realize how long it would take to walk back to my hostel or how tired I would be when I got there.

I slept the first half of the day and spent the evening exploring more of Kutaisi. I was surprised at how much there was to see and how loyal the people here seemed to their city. They treated it like their home, whereas many people I'd met in Tbilisi told me they were from elsewhere. The capital wasn't their home. It was just a place they worked or studied. Yet this city was home to people and to art and culture. The difference in personality and hospitality was easy to see.

INTRODUCTION –

PART TWO: MOONLIT DREAMS

As agreed, I packed my bags and headed to the theater when it got dark. The old man had told me to arrive when the full moon rose over the building. But, not knowing precisely when that might be, I arrived early. Although no one was there, I was content to wait. Anyway, I enjoyed watching the pulse of a city at night. It was the best time to see how honest a place and the people were. So, I took my place and waited.

At first, I didn't see anything or anyone interesting. But as the night passed, couples began to walk by. First, I'd see them going somewhere, and hours later, I would watch as they returned home. I thought one of them might be the person I was supposed to meet, but no one stopped. All the while, the moon crept closer to the theater's roof.

The only thing that ever came and stayed was a perfectly maintained GAZ M-20. But those cars were relics of the Soviet Union, and this one was clearly a taxi.

The driver was an old man who leaned against it smoking hand-rolled cigarettes. Once or twice, I happened to catch his eye, and he'd politely nod and tip his cap each time. But other than those moments, we didn't acknowledge one another.

As the moon crept towards the edges of the sky, I began to realize no one was coming. I might have been more disappointed or surprised than I was, but I didn't feel anything at first. It was like learning you'd lost something or someone you loved. You don't register the pain or accept what you've heard in those first moments. Instead, the knowledge is just a thing. It sits like a stone in your stomach.

I sat there feeling sorry for myself and trying to figure out what I should do next. The old man was gone, and the streets were silent, so I had no hope of taking a taxi anywhere. But then I heard the unmistakable sound of a horse and carriage. My heart jumped in anticipation. This was what I'd been waiting for.

However, what came into view did not meet my expectations. A dirty old white horse rode towards me, pulling a wagon. An even dirtier man and woman were on top of it, sitting next to each other. They rode directly up to me, then got down and started unloading vegetables.

They ignored me while setting up their vegetable stand, and that's when those feelings I mentioned earlier hit me. I was a fool, and this was all some writer's fantasy. Sure, the places were real. Obviously, the story was real too, but I wasn't. I was a foreign thing and didn't belong here. How could I expect to understand something which had existed hundreds of years longer than my country?

Shaking my head at the arrogant tourist I'd allowed myself to become, I looked away from the old couple. I was about to stand and leave when a warm and cheery voice caught my attention. Turning my head, I saw the taxi driver had returned. He had a steaming hot flatbread tucked under one arm and appeared to be haggling with the old couple over the price of vegetables.

As he spoke, he gestured with his other hand. The wheel of cheese draped over his arm swung back and forth like a pendulum while he pointed. Curious to see how this played out, I watched their negotiations with nothing better to do than nurse my bruised ego.

Eventually, they came to an agreement on the price of some tomatoes and cucumbers. Then, in what appeared to be an afterthought, the driver took some spring onions and a head of garlic. Laughing to myself at the thought of his breath and teeth with all that cheese and garlic, I was surprised when he turned and came towards me.

He sat at the opposite end of the bench I was on and placed a small plastic bag next to him. Then he took out a pocketknife and began carving the cheese and vegetables he'd bought. Not wanting to disturb him, I readied myself to leave. But then he tore off a piece of bread and handed it to me before giving me a wink and starting to talk.

"I bet you've traveled half this country and haven't enjoyed your first bit of food like this. Instead, you've probably been busily stuffing yourself with regional delights like khinkali, mtsvadi, and seven kinds of khachapuri. You, tourists, have the worst eating habits. Now, are you going to eat something, or should we sit here until I grow older?"

Then he laughed and started to eat. While chewing, he gestured toward the different buildings around us. As taxi drivers so often do, he told me everything I never needed to know about each place he pointed to. Resigned to my fate, I took him up on his offer and began to eat. A free meal was worth humoring the old guy. Likely he got little business working nights, and his presence gave me something to pass the time with.

To my delight, the food he gave me was one of the best things I'd eaten in Georgia. The tomatoes tasted better than I had eaten before, and the cheese couldn't be compared to anything I knew of. I wondered why this food wasn't served in more restaurants. Or if it was, why I hadn't been told to order it before. But my thoughts were soon interrupted when the driver started speaking again.

"There's a magic, they say, in simple foods, and it doesn't get simpler than this. So, dig in, and let's get going. We've got a long drive."

Looking up from a mouthful of tomato and cheese, my tired brain began processing what he said. This was the man I had been sent to meet! He had been in front of me the whole time, and I was too wrapped up in my own world to notice or pay attention to him.

But these were my last thoughts before a familiar feeling came over me. Once more, the world around me began to fade. Sounds and sights mixed and mingled with the tastes of a foreign yet familiar land, and soon I heard the voices of Avtandil and Phatman...

CHAPTER 01 –

SECRETS OF THE SEA

Avtandil stood before Lady Phatman, his hands and clothes still bloodied. The fire which had overtaken his mind as he slaughtered the guards and wine taster of the Sea Kingdom still tinged his eyes with madness. But there were no threats to him now.

He had made corpses of those who stood in the way of what he wanted. The woman who compelled him to rip the lives from those men was now sworn to speak with him. She had the answers he and Tariel had searched so long to find, and he would be a student to her every word.

"You have slain the man who tried to force my hand against all I love. He who threatened to make me eat my own children. For this, there are no thanks or praise I can give you which will truly encompass the breadth of your service to me. However, I promised to tell you his story, and now I will do so."

With those words, Phatman began her story...

"The city of Gulansharo is unlike any other. We have many unique and wonderful customs. Chief among them is the preservation of New Year's Day. On this most wonderful day, we are given to the remembrance of those we cherish and the ones who care for and protect us."

"No merchants trade their wares, and no one leaves the city. Instead, we prepare ourselves in finery from the first light of morning. Every man and woman dress in their finest clothes. Meanwhile, the lords and rulers of our city prepare a banquet in the castle courtyard."

"Those of us among the great merchant houses are bound by tradition to bring gifts and presents to the court. In turn, the lords must gift us things that are befitting our station and service. We celebrate this event over ten days in total. During this time, the sweet sounds of tambourines and cymbals can be heard everywhere."

"Ball games are played in most public squares, but the main squares are reserved for jousting and feats of strength. Knights charge toward one another on their horses, while acrobats and circus performers show their skills. It is a wonderful experience, and we all look towards this day throughout the year."

"Usen, my husband, is the leader of the great merchant houses, and I lead their wives. To us, all doors are open. There is no place among the rich or poor where we need an invitation. Instead, we come and go as we please, giving presents to all. Of course, for women of our station, our greatest joy is found in the gifts we give the queen."

"Her hand is ever kind to all who inhabit our city. She is both fair and wise but also a lover of fine things. Our time in her court is something we all enjoy, for there are many pleasures to be had. We celebrate with her, taking joy from the steam baths and private gardens. When our time is finished, we return home refreshed of mind and spirit, and full of happiness."

"New Year's Day was no different this year. We came to the queen as was our custom. One and all, we showered her with gifts and rare finery from every place we merchants had traded. And she gave to us until everyone, including her, could receive no more."

"I cannot tell you truthfully what an experience it is, but there is nothing else to compare to any other time of year. We feasted and sipped fine wines until early in the evening. Then we moved to another place as the sun slipped away. There, we continued our celebration."

"I went to the garden with the ladies and had another feast there. My mood was such that I chose to entertain and play with them like a young girl. Minstrels came with us, singing and playing as we danced among ourselves. In time the moon rose. We let down our hair and removed our veils, bathing in its bright pale light."

"Tall and beautiful mansions ringed the garden we sat in. Every one of them was open to us. Some offered views of the sea, while others looked up to the distant mountains ringing the far side of the city. I brought my ladies into the best mansion when we grew tired of our games. On one side, it towered over the sea, with gilded balconies gracefully beckoning to the water like the arms of a lover. On the other side, views of the city and mountains could be had."

"We made yet another feast for ourselves there, surrounded by finery and every sort of food or wine we could want to indulge in. Our conversations were of every sort of thing. Some spoke of men, either young or old, while others discussed women and gossiped about children or matters of court. I entertained them with joy and happiness as if they were sisters."

"Yet, from out of nowhere, a melancholy came over me. I cannot say what it was or from where it originated. In the shadow of my mood, the ladies drifted off to their own designs. Some sought out their loves and lovers, while others returned to the gardens. I could hear them, and though I understood their joy, I could not share it for some reason. Sadness fell over me like soot on the coals of a fire."

"Filled with sorrow, I went to windows overlooking the sea and opened them. Turning my face to the cool night air, I began feeling refreshed. The wind filled my spirit like a sail, renewing the fires of my heart. But, as I stared into the distance, I noticed the smallest thing on the horizon."

"I thought it must be a bird or some beast from the deep. For what else could I have imagined such a thing to be? It was like no ship I had ever seen. The thing seemed to move of its own design, appearing to float over the sea."

"Curious, I watched, hoping to understand what it might be. As it came near, I recognized it as a boat, though I felt it must have sailed from a dream into reality. It shimmered like a pearl under the full moon, and I could see two men standing in it as it got closer. They were black as pitch but large and strong like the warriors of India."

"Yet these men were not like the warriors I had heard tales of. These two were large brutes, coarse and grim in visage, with neither a smile nor laugh shared between them. They stood at either side of the small craft, and as it drew to the edge of the shore, I saw a woman's head appear. I could not contain my surprise at seeing her and wondered what two such men were doing at this hour with a woman on the shores of Gulansharo."

CHAPTER 02 –

THE PEARL OF SORCERY

" I touched this necklace I wear, as you have seen, and summoned the men who serve me, though there were four at that time. However, I was still deciding whether to raise the alarm or go and meet the strangers. Curious, I watched to see what they might do."

"Their boat landed on the beach. Before stepping out, the brutes looked from one side to the other like thieves. I could tell they were wary of who might look upon them, but they could not see me from where I sat. So, I watched in secret, unsure of where the woman had disappeared to."

"Once the men were certain no one could see them, they brought a large chest out from the boat and placed it on the shore. One took a large key from around his neck, and the other some sort of amulet. Together they opened the chest with these items, and the maiden I had seen before stepped out. However, she was much closer this time than when I first saw her."

"About her head and shoulders, a veil and cloak of some strange shimmering material were draped. Beneath these, she wore a torn and stained green silk gown. But these things only caught a moment of my attention, for her beauty captivated every fiber of my being. The sun itself would be happy were it to be like her in beauty."

"As she stepped out of the chest, she turned towards me. I swear to you, rays of light shone from her with such intensity that they reflected from the shore's rocks. Her eyes flashed like distant lightning, illuminating clouds of storms and sorrow behind them. Though I longed to see more of her, I could not keep my eyes on the maiden. It would have been easier to gaze into the sun without blinking."

"Quickly, I closed the curtains over the window to ensure the strange men would not somehow see me. Considering whether to summon the guard or handle the matter myself, I ordered my four men down to the shore. I told them, 'Go down to this woman held captive by these two Indians. Make no sound until you are upon them, but once you are there, see if they will sell her to you. Offer them whatever price they ask, or whatever they may want.'"

"'If they refuse to sell the maiden, do not allow them to take her away. Free her from their clutches and kill them if they try to stop you. Do not let anything or anyone stand in your way. When you have done this, bring her to me.'"

"As you have seen, my men are sorcerers of the Kadj race. They can move without sound and are unlike other men of the earth. This time was no different. In moments they were on the shores of the sea, between the brutes and their boat. Yet those slavers would not sell the girl. They refused any offer of trade or sale."

"However, the men I sent were prepared for this. They

drew their scimitars in unison, forming a ring around the brutes. It was four against two. I expected the battle to end in a moment, but it did not. The slavers were not Indians, as I had thought, but instead were the worst kind of Kadj."

"They fought fiercely, and each was in size equal to two of my men. However, my servants eventually triumphed, cutting the heads from those brutes, and throwing their bodies into the sea. But it was not without cost. Two of my sorcerers were slain, and that moon of a girl was left shaken by the bloodshed."

"Concerned for her, I ran down to the seashore to meet her and soothe her fears. I took her hands and brought her out from the chest, though I could barely look at her. She lit up everything around us with her radiance."

"When I saw her, I knew the sun to be a lie. For there was no power in me to endure her rays. If she had chosen to consume me, I was ready. One needs no preparation when in the presence of an angel."

Phatman stopped speaking then, overcome with emotion at the memory of the woman Avtandil was certain was Nestan. She cried and tore at her hair and cheeks in frustration. A spring of tears ran from her eyes, melting the rose of her brown cheeks. Soon she began shouting at her husband's stupidity and the ignorance of men. But Avtandil soothed her bruised heart. He begged her to continue the story, and she began speaking again.

"I helped her, though to be honest, there was no other choice for me. She had won my every heartbeat with no more than her presence. I brought her back to my chambers and made my heart faithful to her. Whatever comforts and desires she might have had were my only concern. She sat on soft couches, where I caressed and loved her. I kissed every part of her until she grew tired."

"Then I spoke, asking her, 'Oh sun, tell me what race you are or where such beauty has come from. Where were those evil Kadj men taking you? I cannot imagine what they planned to do with a lady of the Pleiades.'"

"But she did not answer me. Whatever I asked, she did not respond. Instead, a hundred springs of tears welled forth from her eyes. They dripped from the raven of her delicate lashes, falling like bits of crystal."

"In time, she calmed, and the press of my questions produced the wine of speech from her lips. Her soft voice shook as she cried, her gentle form swaying like palm fronds in the wind. It was in that moment I knew a fire like no other, and my heart was utterly consumed."

"She only spoke a few words to me, but it was enough. She said, 'You have become dearer than a mother to me. But you do not know what you are asking. What profit will my story be to you? My story is no more than idle gossip on the wind. It is so long since the telling of my tale that it has already been forgotten. I am no more than a lone wanderer, overtaken and consumed by an unhappy fate. Do not ask me of this again or may the might of the All-Seeing curse you!'"

CHAPTER 03 –

What the Sun Cannot Equal

"Such words from one so sweet and gentle as her shocked and surprised me. But I thought, 'Perhaps I ask too much of her and too soon. One should not try to capture the light of heaven and carry it off in the same day. Otherwise, they may go mad and lose their wits entirely.'"

"'Information gathering has a time and a place and must be nurtured with care. An egg does not hatch in one day, nor does a seed grow the moment it is planted. Though I did not know it was too soon to speak with her about these things, now I see clearly. This is not the time or place to converse with this sun.'"

"Realizing she was not ready to speak, I took her hands in mine and led her away. But how does one hide the sun? I knew if I kept her in my home, someone would see her. Then, I had the idea to hide her in one of my other houses. She would be safe from prying eyes there, and I could keep her safe. When I brought her things to eat or sweets and gifts, I could bask in her presence or simply stare into the depths of her beauty."

"My course decided, I dressed her in the heaviest brocades and clothes I had. Things which none could see her form through. Then we waited for the evening when most of the folk would be dining. I carefully took her to a home I rarely visited. It was well-appointed but empty of people. No one came there except me on some occasion or matter of secrecy. This was where I left her and told not a soul."

"For her comfort, I had every sort of thing brought. Whatever I thought she might enjoy was made available to her. Other than me, only my two remaining Kadj servants knew of her existence. We had not even kept that fantastic ship for fear it would raise too many questions. All I had was her, but she was enough."

"However, though I visited often, she did not speak with me. Her behavior was strange, and I could not understand it. Day and night, she wept. An endless stream of tears fell from her eyes, sometimes forming pools at her feet. Though I tried to calm her, nothing I said or did could calm her forlorn heart."

"Instead, my every visit was greeted by the inky black lances of her eyelashes. They jutted out from the jet wells of her eyes. Her cheeks were like new rose buds, bitten by the frost of her tears. The delicate curve of her mouth beckoned me, but the coral and peach of her lips never parted. I did not see the pearls of her teeth within nor receive the bouquet of speech from her mouth."

"The few times I thought she might stop crying, I caused her to start again. To my woe, the questions I tried to ask caused new springs of tears to well forth from her eyes. Because of this, her tears never dried."

"She never revealed the source of her tragedy. So, I stopped asking. I did not believe someone could endure more than whatever had happened to her. Unless perhaps that person was made of stone."

"Her behavior was strange too. She refused any sort of mattress to sleep on. Nor did she accept blankets with which to cover herself. More, she would not even take a pillow. Instead, she rested her head in her arms and slept on the floor."

"Though I might ask a thousand times or more, she barely ate anything. How she did not waste away to nothing is beyond me. I cannot say. More unusual to me was how she dressed. She changed out of the torn and broken green silks I found her in but would not remove the strange veil and short cloak. Though I have seen every kind of rare and costly thing, I cannot tell you what stuff it was made of. The fabric was soft as silk but strong as steel. She was well paired with those strange silks, for they all seemed to be from another world."

"This was how our days passed. One slipped into the next until it seemed there would be no end to them. Yet, she never spoke to me. Meanwhile, I was afraid my husband might discover us, and I did not believe I could trust him. I was sure he would share news of her with everyone in the court if he knew about her. But sooner or later, I knew he would discover my secret."

"Unsure of what else to do, I reasoned that if I told my husband Usen, he might be able to help her. I had no idea what she wanted and did not know what could be done to offer her aid. But if I did not tell him and I was discovered, there would be nothing I could do to save myself or her. He would slay me, and I could not keep her sunlike beauty safe."

"Knowing I could do no more alone, the pain of my inability to help her increased a thousand-fold. I understood I had no choice but to trust Usen, for it would be wrong not to tell my husband. But I would make him swear before God not to betray my secret. If he was willing to give me such assurances, I could be sure he would not doom his soul. Despite his many faults, he was not a breaker of oaths."

"My course was set. I waited until that evening and then went alone to his chambers. I danced for him, playing and frolicking until he was in my hands. Later, when we rested, I made him give me a promise to never share the secret I was about to tell him, and he swore a fearful oath."

"Usen sat up and said, 'May I beat my head on the rocks if I tell a soul what you reveal to me. Into my death, my word shall bind me. Neither those who are old or young nor friend or foe shall ever know what you share with me this night. This is my solemn vow.'"

"Satisfied with his promise and the kindness of his gentle heart, I told him to follow me, and he would see what the sun cannot equal. We stood and dressed, leaving our rooms together."

"With careful steps, we made our way to the house where that mysterious beauty remained hidden. After we came in and shut the door behind us, we went to where she stayed. When his eyes came to rest on her, he forgot all else. His mouth hung open like a fallen gate until he stepped away, pulling me with him."

CHAPTER 04 –

A PENSIVE PANTHER

"He stood outside the door, tightly gripping my arm. Despite the disheveled appearance of the maiden, he was shaking with delight at what he had just seen. Such was the sun's power when contained in an earthly body."

"With a shaking voice, he spoke to me, asking what and who she was. 'Who on earth or in Heaven have you shown me? What have I just seen? Of what stuff is this maiden made of? I swear by my head if she is an earthly being, may God look on me with wrath!'"

"What could I say to my husband? I did not know any more than him. He thought I must have some secret I had not yet shared, so I told him all I knew. 'I don't know more than I have told you. Whether she is a creature of this world, or another is beyond my understanding. Despite asking, she has told me nothing.'"

"'But if we ask her together, we may learn the answer. I have shown her every kindness and mercy. So, perhaps she will tell us who is responsible for the madness afflicting her.'"

"Together, we went back into her chambers, careful to show respect to the maiden. We spoke together, pleading with her. 'You who are a sun to us must realize that a furnace of flames burns our hearts at the sight of you. We must know what has caused the ruby of your heart to become so blue. Tell us, please. For in your words rests a balm for our souls and a cure to the waning moon.'"

"But we could not tell if she listened or even heard us. Her back was turned, and the rose of her lips remained glued shut, concealing the pearls therein. The locks of her ebony hair were haphazardly twined together like serpents."

"We would have liked to see the light of her face. Yet the garden of her soul was built against us. The smoke of a hundred dragons eclipsed her brightness. Only darkness greeted our pleas for her to shine the gift of speech over us."

"Though she was silent, a storm stirred within her, but we did not see it. There was no sign. How could we have known? Instead, we poked and prodded with our conversation, annoying the panther we didn't realize she had become. Until, at last, something broke within her."

"She turned towards us, fire blazing in her eyes. For a moment, we were afraid, but then the dam within her broke. Rivers of tears poured from her eyes as sobs wracked her body. She shouted at us before collapsing in a heap, 'I do not know! Now leave me alone!'"

"We could not comprehend the tragedy our words caused her to become. Her grief was so intense we were also drawn into it, falling beside her. Each of us left crying and apologizing for what harm our ignorance had caused. Yet nothing we did soothed the hurt tormenting her soul."

"When at last her tears stopped, she refused to move

from where she fell. Instead, she sat like that for hours. Though we tried to feed her with bits of fruit, our every effort was refused."

"Unsure of what to do, we retreated a few steps from her. I sat next to my husband on one of the couches the maiden had never used, but I said nothing more to her. What could I have said that she had not already heard from my lips?"

"After some time, Usen spoke to me. 'Just the sight of her has wiped countless woes from my heart. Looking at her, I feel a portion of my youth returned to me. But what is she? Her cheeks are only fit to receive the sun.'"

"'How could any man dare to think of kissing them? Had I never seen her, I would not realize how much I have suffered in this life. And now the sight of her has cured this malaise I was unaware of. I tell you, if I prefer my own children to her, may God slay them!'"

"He spoke, as men often do when they should not, and his words cut me. But I could not disagree with him. Save the joy I held at the sight of my own children, no one ever lit my spirit as this maiden had."

"The two of us sat there gazing at her for longer than I can count. We wished for some sign or word, but she gave none. Eventually, we left, abandoning the joy of her presence and suffering the grief of parting."

"Each of us continued our lives as normal. Though, what once brought joy became routine without seeing the maiden. Any time we were free from the affairs of trade, we went to see her. It was as though our hearts were woven into the threads of her Fate. We were imprisoned in the net of her tragedy until it became our own."

"The nights and days of our life were sped up because of this. It seemed one day passed when a span of five was gone. When we understood this, it was a shock to us both. Neither my husband nor I could believe how he had forgotten the King, and I abandoned the ladies of our community."

"It had been almost three weeks since we attended court duties. I could easily make amends with the ladies, but Usen could not. He was the King's man and must be present more often than he had been."

CHAPTER 05 –

THE TONGUE OF A FOOL

"Realizing the mistake of his absence, Usen readied himself to visit the King. He gathered a tray of black and white pearls with hurried hands, mixing in many different colored gems. And then he went up to prepare himself with fresh clothes and perfumes."

"But I grew concerned. What if he talked? I knew him well. Despite his flaws, he was still my husband. Like the King, he was a wine lover. The two often drank into the early morning hours, boasting and promising impossible things to one another. I had no doubt wine would loosen his tongue like the belt of a man fattening himself on full means after returning from a voyage at sea."

"I shared my thoughts when he came back down and made him swear a vow to say nothing to anyone. He swore to God on the Holy Koran that swords should strike his head if he dared speak of the maiden. This was good enough for me. I trusted his word, for despite his flaws, he was honest."

"He left then and made his way to court. The King was feasting there with his friends, but when he saw Usen, he immediately called him over. You see, my husband is not only the chief merchant but also the man our King likes best to drink with. The two are dear friends and often fill their cups together until the wine runs from them."

"Sometimes their toasts are put into verse and poetry by our minstrels. On other days, the court jesters make their words into uproarious jokes. But this day, the King smiled. He received the gifts Usen brought with a smile and a laugh, for they were a joy and a delight to behold."

"As was their tradition, soon the two of them were deep in their cups. From goblets of wine to tankards of ale, they drank. Soon beakers of spirits were brought forth, and the truth of my ill-bred and rash husband shone through."

"Usen forgot his oaths and promises. For, what are Korans and Meccas to a tipsy merchant who has lost himself in the spirits of distilled grapes and fruits? This is why wise men say a rose does not befit a crow, and horns are unsuited to donkeys."

"There they sat, dare I say it, crow and donkey, drunk as they were. The King commended Usen, clapping him on the back as he raised a toast. 'Ever do I wonder where you get these fine gems. How do you find such pearls as these and rubies the size of a hen's egg? By my head, were I to return one-tenth of the gifts you present me, I would empty the coffers of my Kingdom!'"

"Usen stood, swaying like a toddler just learning to walk, and answered, cup held high. 'Lord, you who are mightier than any here, I salute you. You shine brightly upon us and nourish those who enjoy the light of your presence. What do I have in my hands, and who does it truly belong to? I will tell you! Whatever gold or treasure can be called mine, and even my own children, have been granted to me by you.'"

"'More, let me be bold in my words and say these gifts I have given are unbefitting one such as you. My gratitude cannot be shown with such baubles! There is a secret thing I possess, brighter than any sun. She is more lovely than the daughter of the moon.'"

"'When you see her, your thanks will be greater than any sea, for you will understand my devotion to you. Make a bride of her and unite her with your son. I promise you, no King in the world has ever had a daughter-in-law more beautiful than her!'"

"What more should I say? There is no point in lengthening my speech. Usen broke his oaths to God and to me. He told everyone at court about the maiden."

"Of course, the King was greatly pleased. His heart leaped with joy at the idea of such a bride for his son, though I'm sure he hardly believed half of what my husband said about the maiden. He knew the boasts and claims the two made to each other."

"Still, he wanted to show respect for his friend. Because of this, he ordered her brought to court. Moreover, a celebration was made in honor of my husband for the rash promise he had made."

CHAPTER 06 –

A GATHERING OF SHADOWS

"For myself, I had no knowledge of these events. When my door opened, I was sitting at home, pleasantly attending to my affairs. Before me stood the Chief of the King's Guard."

"Sixty soldiers filled the courtyard behind him. They came in without any invitation, as is customary and permitted by their station. I was quite surprised, unsure whether some great thing had happened."

"What matter of state could compel these men into my home at this late hour? Little did I know how soon I would learn the truth of their visit. For the Chief addressed me."

"'Lady Phatman, I come at the command of our King, who is equal to the sun. He orders the maiden, who shines like double suns, to be brought before him. You must bring her to me now, and I shall escort her to the palace.'"

"When I heard his words, I knew immediately what had happened and of whom he spoke. Heaven spun above my head, threatening the earth I stood on. And an earthquake of wrath boiled in my soul."

"Hoping against hope at the possibility of some mistake, I asked who they sought. But any reprieve I might have wished for was dashed to pieces at his response. The Chief told me Usen promised a maiden to the King. One with a face flashed with lightning, who outshone the sun."

"I could do nothing. No power on earth could enable me to stop the Chief, let alone escape sixty of the King's finest guardsmen. Unable to take a step forward or to sit down, I asked the soldiers to wait while I fetched her. I told them it was unseemly for men to walk in on such a woman, to which they agreed."

"Then I went to her, that lovely angel. She sat alone in her bath of tears and did not look up when I came in. With no choice, I told her of what had happened."

"'Oh, my sweet sun, it seems Fate forever betrays us all. Though I tried to protect you, Heaven has turned against me. The ashes of all I hoped for rain down upon my head like a funeral pyre. My heart breaks, for the King has come to take you. I am sorry, but however much this uproots my soul and despoils my heart, there is nothing I can do. You must go to him.'"

"And then, a ray of light broke through the clouds. Until then, her every moment with me had been darkened by whatever sorrow she carried. Yet, at that moment, she shone more beautifully than I had ever seen. She gifted me with her speech. Though I wish her words had been any other than those she spoke."

"'Sister, do not be surprised at the darkness of events. Did I not first tell you how I am afflicted? Fate is a luckless and treacherous witch who has forever done ill to me. However difficult this may be for you, do not despair of yourself on my account.'"

"'Had some justice or good been done to me, it would be fitting of you to marvel at the wonder. But this, what is it to me? Only another evil to pile on the heap of woe I carry in my soul. This is not new. No, for me, such things are so common as to seem meaningless.'"

"Then she began to cry. Delicate tears spilled down her face like water falling from the edge of a lily. Yet her back remained straight, and I could see the resolve in her heart."

"She stood, fearless as a panther. There was no joy in her eyes, nor was there any trace of woe. All she asked of me was to cover her form and face with the veils she wore."

"Yet, I could not so easily abandon this bird who had fallen from her nest and into my care. I begged her to wait a moment and ran to our treasury. From there, I took gems and pearls of which no price could be set. Each one was worth a small city, but I did not care for their value then or now. All I cared for was her. What was most valuable to us, I prepared."

"When I returned, I wrapped these treasures around her waist before hiding them beneath the veils and robes she asked for. I advised her to keep these things hidden. Perhaps they might give her some hope or chance where it seemed my hand had been unable to."

"Then I led her out. She came with neither sigh nor groan, like an albatross fallen from Heaven. Yet those to whom I handed her over to were unaware of this. Only I knew how she felt inside, for she had only spoken to me. Though, giving her to the King's men left my heart feeling like it had died."

CHAPTER 07 -

A CELEBRATION OF RUIN

" I followed the Chief and his soldiers as they took her. When they came before the King, he uncovered her face. To my surprise, I saw she had not a single tear. Neither was there any smile."

"But the light of her being could not be contained. Wherever she was paraded, she went with her head bowed, saying not a word. Nor did she look directly at anyone there."

"Meanwhile, huge kettle drums around the city were beaten slowly and steadily. This was typical of Gulansharo to announce a great event. People came from every corner of the city to see what was happening. Word of her beauty spread like wildfire. Onlookers rushed over the officers to see her, trampling one another as they pressed forward."

"Those who stared too long at her form were forced to blink as if blinded by sunlight. Even the King could not contain his amazement. He compared her approach to the sun coming down from Heaven to grace his court. His words echoed above the din of those gathered, 'Many are the sights I have seen in this world, and endless the pleasures I have known. Yet who other than God could imagine one such as this woman before us? Those who are in love with her and cannot find succor are right in their wretchedness by roaming mad in the desert!'"

"When the Chief and his men finished parading the maiden around the courtyard, they seated her beside the King. He looked at her long before speaking. 'Fairest of the fair, I must ask who you are and to whom you belong? What is your race, and where have you come from?'"

"However, the maiden said nothing. Of her sun-like face, no sign of her thoughts could be detected. Instead of answering, she bowed her head. Though she did not engage in discourse with any, she remained gentle, sitting with sorrow draped about her."

"Whatever the King said, she did not respond or acknowledge him. The rose of her lips remained sealed, and the treasure of pearls therein was not revealed. Her heart was elsewhere, and she thought of another."

"Those who looked at her did not know this, though. Instead, they wondered what she thought and why she would not speak. None had harmed her or done any wrong. But she remained silent. There were no words from her lips."

"After a time, the King spoke again. He addressed the matter of her silence. 'What must we think of this one who chooses not to speak with us? Where can we draw comfort for our hearts so scorched by the brightness of this beauty before us? The silence of this maiden leaves me with two minds, and I think there can no other possibilities. First, she may be in love with someone else. The thoughts she does not share are those that forever turn toward her beloved. In this case, she has no desire for any other, and so speaks to no one.'"

"'Another possibility may be that she is a sage. Her mind is not like ours. What she sees is above us, lofty and high as the gates of Heaven. To her, there is no joy or sorrow. Neither does she find happiness or misfortune. Everything is the same to her, so no things are of consequence. Her spirit soars where ours cannot travel, and so her mind is like that of a dove.'"

"'Whatever she is, I will have her ready for the return of my son – may God grant him victory and a speedy return to Gulansharo. Perhaps he will draw the bouquet of speech from her lips or cause the pearls therein to shine with a smile. Then we shall also know of this maiden and what her secrets are. Until that time, let us put her away. She will rest like the waning moon until the sun of our Kingdom returns.'"

"Now, lest you think the son of our King is a bad man, I will tell you of him. He is a good youth, fair in form and face. Among the Knights of our Kingdom, he is peerless in valor and beauty and fearless in combat. None are the equal of this Hero, and he is beloved of the people."

"For many moons, he has been away at war to the west, fighting what remains of the empire of Axum. They once ruled these lands and were similar in skill to the Kadjis. But the First King of our Gulansharo defeated them. There are few left, but they are still a threat to us. This youth, who will return, is who they prepared the maiden to meet."

"But I digress. Let us return to the mysterious maiden. Maidservants took her away at the King's order. They bathed her, scrubbing away the outward signs of sorrow. Her hair was done in finery, and then they draped jeweled gowns about her."

"Gems and precious stones glittered from every part of

her. Then they placed a crown of pure ruby on her head. It complimented the glow of her freshly washed face and caused her rays to shine with renewed intensity. Still, she did not speak."

"While the maiden was being prepared, the King ordered the Royal Chambers of the Princess furnished. A peerless couch of gold was placed therein, imported from the west, and covered in a deep red fabric. When she was ready, the King accompanied her as she was escorted to the rooms."

"To guard her, he left nine eunuchs. Then he departed and returned to celebrate at the feast prepared in honor of this maiden who was brighter than the sun. Once more, the huge drums were beaten, summoning people to the palace."

"My husband Usen was the guest of honor. He received countless gifts more valuable than anything we had ever owned. This was his reward for the service he had rendered to the King. Trumpets sounded, and minstrels sang. Everyone there was joyous, except for me."

"My joy rested in the Fate of the girl I had rescued. Yet, I feared what would become of her. Lost to my sorrow, I claimed to feel ill and returned to my home while others celebrated the ruin I mourned."

CHAPTER 08 –

THE CROWN OF TEMPTATION

"Unbeknownst to me, the maiden was familiar with such celebrations and royalty. She knew how long the Lords and Ladies would be at their cups. Yet she could not escape and so cursed her plight."

"'What a murderous witch Fate is, and I am forced to suffer her ills. She has cast me from one treachery to another. I do not know who these strange people are or what lands I have come to.'"

"'Nor can I say for whose sake I am mad now. The man I love has not come to rescue me. So, what can I do, and who can I trust myself to? I swear, this life is not one I would choose for an enemy, yet it seems I have no recourse.'"

"'I cannot think of what might avail me or the road I must take, but I will not wither here! Perhaps God will see fit to protect me. For what reasonable person slays themselves before death comes? When one is in trouble, they must not lose their wits. So, I will make my way from here in whatever way I can.'"

"Thinking of what to do, she called the eunuchs to her and spoke to them. 'You who stand guard over me, come, for I would speak to you. It is treachery and deception to which you and your King have all fallen. I am no princess. Nor am I royalty. Your Lord is mistaken in wishing me as a bride for his son.'"

"'He sounds the trumpets and celebrates in vain, for I am not suited to be your queen. My path lies elsewhere; I do not desire any man, however good or well-formed he may be! What you ask of me is far from my desire, and this life becomes bitter to me!'"

"'Should you keep me here, I will kill myself. Your King will blame you for this, and your lives will be forfeit, no different than my own, though for another reason. Your time in this world will end. You will sacrifice every joy you have had. And for what?'"

"'Is it not better for you to take these treasures I wear and leave me to my freedom? Who among you would not regret the liberty these jewels can buy? Are they not better than a life to be brought to an early end by the wrath of your King?'"

"With those words, she removed the gems and pearls about her waist, all of it wreathed in gold. She took the crown of ruby from her head and gave it to those who stood guard over her freedom. Once more, she begged them, 'Take these baubles, for none of us will benefit from them if we are dead. My heart burns and aches for my freedom. Give me this in exchange for these treasures, and may God forever bless your path in life.'"

"Real treasure causes a strange affliction in men and women alike. Often have I seen this myself. Even the wealthy are sometimes tempted to throw away life and liberty for treasures. Yet to those who have nothing, the possibility of such wealth drives them to madness. The eunuchs were no different."

"Seeing the jewels and gems dangled just beyond their reach drove them into a frenzy. Lust for what she held caused each man there to forget his duty to King and Kingdom. Instead, each thought of what he could gain, imagining a life bought differently than the one they had now. As one, those men agreed to help her escape. Such is the power of gold."

"But to those who love gold, it gives no joy. They gnash their teeth and count coins until the day of their death. And all the while, gold comes in and out like the tide. Yet those who crave wealth don't realize this."

"They blame the heavens and planets and call on astrologists and seers when they have not. Never realizing it binds the soul to this world and keeps it from soaring to Heaven. But the eunuchs did not know this, so they could not consider it."

"Instead, they held out eager hands for what she had in abundance, and they had not. One man removed his garments and helped her dress so none would recognize her. Then they all went out through other exits from the palace. For the great halls and courtyards were full of drunken people celebrating. They could not safely pass there."

"Once they left the castle, the eunuchs disappeared into the dark, and the maiden made her way to another place. She had no trouble picking her steps, for the moon was full. It had not yet been swallowed by the serpent of darkness."

"Unbeknownst to me, the place she went was my home. I heard a soft knock at the door but was not bothered to answer it. Presumably, someone called me to rejoin the revelry at court, but I had no spirit for it. Yet, when one of my servants told me about a maiden in strange clothes and covered face asking for me, I instantly knew who it was."

"Immediately, I embraced her, overcome with surprise and joy. I asked her to come in, but she looked confused and asked why I had invited her in. Truly, I must tell you, her refusal to enter my home at that moment drove a lance through my heart. But she explained what happened, and I understood her reasons."

"'My freedom has been bought with the riches you gave me and those your King adorned me with. I pray to God that he will reward you in Heaven for what you have done, but I cannot stay here. If you hide me, the men of your Kingdom will discover us both, and Fate will ruin the way for me once more.'"

"'I beg of you, lend me a horse. This way, I might flee before the King learns of my escape. Please, help me with this one final thing. Let me go before he sends men in pursuit of me.'"

"She spoke the truth, which I could not deny. I led her to my stables in secret and saddled our best steed. Once she sat on its back, she smiled for the first time. It was better to me than the seeing lights of Heaven mounting the lion of Leo."

"She left, and I saw no more of her save those veils she forever wore as they disappeared into the night. I felt the best of my labor was lost that day. But I said nothing to anyone. Instead, I waited."

CHAPTER 09 –

THE GRAPES OF WRATH

"Night grew into day and again into the night. Rumors spread through the Kingdom of the missing maiden. Within the city, an alarm had been raised. It was as though we were under siege. Armed men roamed the streets, and every home was searched."

"Initially, I thought it was a simple search, but I was wrong. The King sent men who were after blood. Any who hid her or knew her whereabouts but did not speak of them would be executed. When they came to my house and asked, I pleaded my innocence to them and begged them to search themselves, lest any speak ill of me."

"For two nights, they scoured the city for her. Meanwhile, fast riders had been sent to find word of her passing. To my secret joy, none found her or news of where she may have gone. I could only hope for her safety."

"For a month after, all the Kingdom wore the color

violet. They mourned her, who had appeared to vanish. All who had seen her lamented the loss of what a sun she had been to them. Their sorrow was no different than my own. Yet among them all, only I knew the truth."

"Though you may not believe it, I learned where she had gone and what Fate befell her. But first, I must give what you asked for, which is why that man threatened to make me eat my children. You have heard about how my husband betrayed me, so I will start with that."

"I am sure it will not surprise you to learn I was unsatisfied with him. He is lean and ill-favored, which love blinded me to when I was a maid. But time removes the shine from the most ardent of love."

"Ours was no different, though I would not have betrayed him except for one thing. He broke his oaths to me when he told of the maiden. I have never forgiven him for that. Nor will I."

"Because of this, I sought another love. Many ladies in our court have men like this. It seemed to me a satisfying way to pass the time. My mistake was to become the doe of a wicked man and allow him to be my buck."

"For timidity slurs a man, and wantonness a woman. Yet, the man I chose occupied a high role in the Kingdom. I thought he was of better character."

"He was the Chachnagir, a gentleman high in the court, responsible for selecting the best wines. His past was unknown to me, but it did not matter. I believed we loved one another, and our time together was pleasant. That is until I unknowingly invited him to show me the kind of man he really was."

"In truth, the fault was my own. I was stupid and unwise, behaving like a young maiden before her first kiss. Like a fool, I told him the same story you just heard and spared no detail."

"He learned every bit of how the maiden came to me.

More, I told him of my help in her escape. I thought he was my friend, but it turned out differently. He made himself a foe to me, menacing my every move."

"If I spoke to another man, even in business, he became insanely jealous. Soon he threatened me with exposure. There was nothing I could do against him. He came to me whenever he wanted, forcing himself on me in any way and time he wished. "

"Now, when I think of him as a corpse, it is with relief. I will not mourn his passing. Rather, I would prefer a cup of his blood to drink for what he did to me. My heart still tells me he deserved worse. But as it was not my hand which did the deed, it is enough to know his corpse feeds the fish."

"But you must know, I was not careless when inviting you to my bed. I did not realize that evil man was in the city when I called you. Then, after I had invited you, he told me I must see him. Although I tried to keep you from coming, you would not turn away."

"And when I saw you, I could not resist the light of your form and strength of your arms. At that moment, nothing but you mattered to me. How could I say no to what I so badly wanted and needed?"

"But then he came in with his man, and I feared the two of you would fight. I could think of nothing to say or any way to stop him. Yet it was me he wished dead, not you. Otherwise, he would have fought you then."

"And if you had not fought him, he would have informed the entire court of my aid to the maiden. I would have been ruined, and my house destroyed with one swipe of the King's hand. Then, as Kuru promised, he would have suggested I eat my own children as punishment."

"In his anger, the King would have agreed. My poor babies would have been slaughtered. Then they would have stoned me to death for my infidelity, and all my house would have been brought to ruin."

"Now, I can ask no more from God other than His eternal reward to you for what you have done. Your hand spared my children and me a Fate worse than death. You have safely delivered us from the serpent's gaze. We are free of the evil that man would have wrought, and I no longer need to fear death at his hands. Once more, the stars shine brightly on me, and I have you to thank for this!"

Avtandil thought long on what she told him. He was sure the woman in her story was Nestan. Though, it was clear Phatman did not know the maiden's name. However, much to his delight, she had mentioned knowing where the maid went.

This was the information he needed. He soothed Phatman's shaken, praising her with gentle words. Then asked for more information about the maiden.

"Do not fear what has passed. The evil of that man is gone. He can never disturb you again. But surely you must know it is written in the Book that the most hateful of foes are the ones who pretend to be a friend. Yet those who are wise do not easily confide, even amongst friends. However, your worry is gone now. He is a corpse."

"Though, I must ask more of your story, for you left the tale unfinished. You said there was further news of the maiden but did not share it. Tell me, what is it you learned of her Fate?"

When he asked about the further journeys of the maiden, Phatman was silent for many minutes. Then, she began to weep. But with hesitant and pained words, she began to speak once more.

CHAPTER 10 –

THE KING'S DEATH

With tears nesting in the corners of her eyes, Phatman began to speak of Fate. The evil witch and false betrayer of vows, which she said could only be compared to the Prince of Darkness. The Lord of evil, thrown from Heaven, and whose treachery none can know or predict. Then she lamented life and all the vanities we harbor.

Phatman cried over every person who ever hoped for a reprieve from the desolation which eventually embraced us all. At last, her words turned to the maiden's story. Avtandil turned his full attention to the tale she told, becoming a student to her every word.

"It may pain you to know she was brought to nothing. The ray of the sun, which illuminated the darkness of my life, is forever gone from us. She cannot be saved, this one who increased the breadth of my hands and all I do."

"Our sweet angel still burns me with fires even my

sorrow cannot quench. But I must start this story from the beginning. Otherwise, the pace of her tragedy may confuse the telling of how she came to an end."

"When she first left, I lost myself to a deep depression. My house and children became hateful things to me. Each day I woke to a graveyard of sorrow consuming my heart. Her Fate was always on my mind from when I woke until I slept."

"But even my dreams brought the memory of her back to me. I could not escape my pain and worry. Nor was I able to stomach the sight of my husband. Usen, that faithless breaker of oath and infidel to God."

"His every approach was refused by me. Nearness to him was like a plague. I stayed far from him. His cursed face was something I had no desire to see."

"But it happened that one day I was walking at the edge of the city. The sun was setting, and I hoped for some joy from the sight. With each step, I cursed the vows of every man who has ever walked this earth. Yet, my sorrow would not depart. It seemed that loss and pain would forever be my companions."

"As I passed the guards at the gates, I saw a wayfarer enter the city with three other men. He was dressed like a servant, but his companions wore the garb of men well accustomed to the road. They were eating and drinking, merrily discussing their travels with one another. Curious, I listened to what they said."

"They first talked of their joy at resting after having traveled from this place or that. Each told stories of the difficulties they experienced on the road. Soon, I realized they could not be companions or their tales would not be so different and varied."

"True to what I observed, they soon bragged about their travels and adventures. Each man jokingly contested the other, claiming his path was more difficult or his deed of greater valor. But I soon grew bored with listening to them. Such chatter is idle and meaningless."

"I turned to walk away, but the words of the man dressed like a servant caught my ears, and I stopped. What he said was different than the other men. I listened intently to him, curious about who he was and where he came from."

"'Brothers, you have sown no more than seeds with the deeds you speak of. Yet, I harvest pearls through mine! I tell you this. Providence is from He on high, in the Kingdom of the Celestials. It is from there my tale originates. Listen, and I will enlighten you, for my story is better by far than the sum of all you have said!'"

"'I was most recently a slave, having been forced into servitude of the King who rules over the Kadjis. Yet some years ago, a sickness fell on him. Though, even now, none outside the Kingdom of Kadjeti know of this. He who gave life to his people could not overcome the shadow of the underworld. Illness overtook him, and his spirit departed.'"

"'The King's death left his children orphaned, and their care fell to his sister Dulardukht. Now she raises her dead brother's children, the eldest who will one day sit on the throne. But it is she who rules Kadjeti.'"

"'Those who have tasted the bite of her wrath call her Dulardukht the Mighty, the Witch Queen of Kadjeti. And woe to those who cross her. Though she is a woman, her demeanor is like that of a rock. One might more easily approach the face of a cliff than speak with her.'"

"'She keeps one slave above all others. His name is Roshak, and he is also of the Kadj race. Because of this, he has his own magic. This makes him chief among those like us who are not Kadjis. Though he is a slave, he enjoys a freedom no other slave has.'"

"'While she issues his orders, he sometimes goes away

on his own, attacking this way or that. No one has ever been able to hurt him, but there are many he wounds, for he has an army of several thousand other slaves. Those he meets are utterly ruined. In this way, he increases the Queen's glory and the Kadj Empire's reputation. Because of this, she allows him this freedom.'"

"'However, not long after the King's death, we learned his wife had also died. She was dearer than a sister to Dulardukht, for they had grown together from childhood. This news left Queen's nephews Rosan and Rodia without a mother or father.'"

"'However, this news came to us from across the sea, from the fortress of Alamut. It greatly disturbed our advisors, who debated how they would tell the Queen of her loss. Roshak overheard their words and grew angry with what he viewed as the impotence of the wise men.'"

"'Arrogant as he was, he refused to be in the city when the mourning started. He did not care if he was killed for his disrespect. All he desired was the blood of innocents and conquest in the name of his Queen.'"

"'Determined to go into the fields and bring ruin to those he met, he chose a hundred of us from his slaves. We were commanded to accompany him. Our purpose would be to enslave others and take what they held to enrich our Kingdom.'"

"'We left at his order, each of us armed and ready to make war on those we met. Others would come behind us to carry whatever goods we looted and lead chains of captives back to the mines of Kadjeti. By day we sought quarry, and at night we watched for fires of the unwary. Many caravans fell to us. We looted their wares and chained the merchants, sending them back as slaves.'"

CHAPTER 11 –

THE VOICE OF THE MOON

"But Roshak was no fool. He knew the Queen would cross over sea and mountains to the far lands of Alamut to mourn her sister. For this reason, he would return to Kadjeti before she left, pretending he hadn't known of her loss. This way, he could enrich himself before being forced to accompany her on the long journey of mourning.'"

"'It so happened that we saw a great light shining from a nearby field on one very dark night when the moon was new. Some thought it was dawn, while others believed the sun had fallen from Heaven. Several men feared what it might be, whispering of Devis and supernatural beings. For, as everyone knows, Kadji and Devi are the sworn enemies of one another.'"

"'We arranged our weapons and prepared for battle, forming a wide circle around whatever the thing might be. Then, from the midst of the light, a high and sweet voice came to us. Though at first, we could not say whether it was a youth or a lady.'"

"'The voice addressed us as Knights, asking for our names and what we were doing on the plains. We were warier now of Devi magic than before. There is power in names, and none know this better than the Devis. But the voice continued speaking and told us they had come from Gulansharo with a message for the King of Kadjeti.'"

"'We came closer when we heard this, and a sun-faced rider appeared from the midst of the light. The brilliance of the rider's face flashed like lightning, spreading itself over us and all we stood on. Words came to us again from the radiant being, and we saw it was a lady of incomparable beauty. When we saw her smile, the jet of her lashes left many among us heart slain.'"

"'But she did not fool us. We knew she spoke falsely, for there has never been a slave like her. This was clear to us. And when Roshak understood it was a maiden who spoke, he rode to her side and laid hands on her. I did not know what he might do with her, but I was certain it would not be pleasant.'"

"'When he seized her, she understood the loss of her freedom and began to weep. Her presence's light faded, and the serpent ate the moon once more. Darkness seeped back in like the tide filling a swamp. But no matter how many questions we asked, she did not speak again. It was as if by laying hands on her, we had extinguished that which gave her light and life.'"

"'Roshak brought her to our camp, and we tried without success to coax her to speak again. We asked who she was and how she had become to be alone and on the plains. Surely no one ever left a gem like her to waste away to nothing in the fields. But for all our pressing questions, we only received her anger. Like an asp, her eyes and manner attacked us. We dared not look too long on her for fear of what magic or curses she might contrive against us.'"

"'However, Roshak was unmoved by her or the threat of her eyes. He told us to stop questioning her, for there was no purpose in shouting down a well. Whatever her business was no longer mattered. She would be presented to the Queen. It was known that our Sovereign enjoyed the good fortune of receiving whatever she wanted from God. Though none knew how this was.'"

"'More importantly, had we wanted to keep the damsel to ourselves, it would be an ill thing. The Witch Queen is proud. To hide such a thing from her would be a great disgrace. She would take offense, and none of us would see the light of day again.'"

"'But that was not all. In bringing the maiden as a gift for the Queen, Roshak would be rewarded. And what rewards he received, we also sometimes enjoyed. Because of this, the conquests we had planned were shortened. Instead of preying on those who traveled the roads, we returned to Kadjeti with the maiden.'"

"'However, I did not accompany them. Instead, I asked Roshak if it might be wise to visit Gulansharo and ask if any here knew about the girl. But he was too busy preparing to return to Kadjeti. He paid little attention to me or my request, dismissing me. And now I am here.'"

"'I know he will be gone for at least a year, which means there is no possibility of anyone from Kadjeti finding me if I do not return. The only question is what I will do, for my road diverges here, and I am still determining which path to take. One is well-trodden and returns me to Kadjeti and a lifetime of servitude. While the other will lead to freedom, which I have not enjoyed in so long the taste is foreign to me.'"

"'I carry pearls of treasure, knowledge, and years of wisdom in my hands. Yet, the question of what difference there is between a slave and a servant haunts me. All are subject to a master other than themselves. This is the reason my path remains uncertain.'"

"'On either side of me, an abyss stretches deeper than I can see. Will I be my own slave or return to the chains I have only just escaped? I cannot say yet, but I am sure the tale I told is better by far than those you shared!'"

"With these words, the man started laughing. Soon, the other men began to laugh with him. They were greatly pleased by the story he told them. And I could see them wondering at the wisdom he shared when his tale had finished. But his words were not what caught my interest. It was the maiden he described which drew my attention."

"I was certain it was her who I longed to know of. My tears dried at once, and my curiosity grew. With some impatience, I waited for the man to be alone."

CHAPTER 12 -

NO HOPE HANGS HERE

"When the four men finished eating and drinking, they went their separate ways. I waited a bit behind and then followed the slave from Kadjeti. When there was no one around, I announced myself to him."

"Taking him by the arm, I asked him to tell me again what he said to the other men. He related the same story, and it renewed the life I had thought lost after the departure of the maiden. I pressed a coin into his hand and thanked him for his service to me."

"When he left, I called the two Kadji servants left to me. The same two sorcerers who you have seen, one of which guided you to the place where you ended Kurva's life. In the way of every Kadj, they could come and go without being seen. Because of this talent, I sent them to Kadjeti to learn what they could of the maiden."

"Though I worried over what might happen to them if they were caught, my need for knowledge of her was greater than any other concern I might have had. From one day to the next, I waited. I gnashed my teeth and tore at my hair, pacing my home and worrying over any sign of news."

"On the third day, to my surprise, my vigil was rewarded. The two men I sent had returned. They brought information with them, and I listened eagerly."

"I learned the Witch Queen of Kadjeti had taken the maiden and betrothed her to the little boy Rosan. This was the order and decree of Dulardukht. However, she could not oversee the wedding until her sister's mourning time passed. The journey to the fortress city of Alamut would require crossing over sea and mountains and then back again."

"It was no easy journey, and the Queen would be gone for at least one year in mourning for her sister. While she was gone, she ordered that none were to look on the maiden. Whether because no one could look at her sun-like brightness or because she feared someone would try to spirit her away from that place, my sorcerers could not say. But they were clear about the Queen leaving for the distant lands of Alamut."

"She would return home when her heart was not consumed with grief. Then, she would celebrate the wedding of young Prince Rosen and make a daughter-in-law of Heaven's sun. Until that time, the girl is locked away in the castle's highest tower. Only a single eunuch attends to her needs. She sees no other than him."

"As concerns Dulardukht, the Witch Queen of Kadjeti, I have already told you of the long and perilous road she must travel. But there is more. Many are her enemies and those who were enemies of her sister. No small number of men will try to overcome the Queen through force of arms, but I am sure they will fail."

"She will have taken her most skilled sorcerers with

her. Undoubtedly, she also travels with a company of Knights. No one will surprise her, and no others possess sorcery to equal that of the Kadj race."

"In her absence, countless warriors remain to protect Kadjeti Castle from assault. Though she will be gone for one year, no foe has ever breached the walls of that fortress. It is hewn from stone, as if by the magical arts of Devis."

"To reach the tower the maiden is in, one must breach the gates, which are guarded by ten thousand Knights. But to get there, they must first climb a long hollowed-out passage to reach the castle. But before that, there are the outer walls, with three massive gates."

"Each of those gates has another three thousand men standing guard. So, to reach the castle's tallest tower, where the star of Heaven is locked away, one must overcome impossible odds. There is no way she might contrive her escape. But even if she did, I do not know she would go."

"Do you see now why I say she is lost? There is no hope of rescuing her. And once Queen Dulardukht returns and breaks her will, she will willingly wed the young Prince Rosan. The light which sets her apart from the world will dim. Though her body may live on, all she was will have died with the loss of her freedom."

CHAPTER 13 –

To Kill a Kadji

Avtandil listened to all Phatman said. Though the tale she spun was filled with woe, he was pleased to hear of Nestan. Realizing he was so close to what he sought brought joy to his heart. It eased the suffering he had endured so long. He thanked her, for what she gave him was no small thing, though she did not know this yet.

"You are truly beloved and worthy of being loved by me. How your words stir and agitate the still sands of my inner soul. I would welcome more news of these Kadjis. What can you tell me of the lands of Kadjeti? If they are such monsters, how can they be called human?"

"I cannot understand them, but pity for the maiden kindles a fire in me. What could they possibly want with a woman! We both know how terrible men can be toward those of the fairer sex. But if these Kadjis are not the same as normal men, it pains me to imagine the evil those sorcerous monsters may have planned for the poor girl."

Phatman laughed when he said this and then apologized when she saw the severe expression on his face. She had forgotten he knew nothing of those of the Kadj race. So, he did not understand their nature. With a smile, she rested her hand on his and began to explain.

"I am sorry to have confused you. The Kadjis are human men and women. However, they are different from us. They trust steep rocks, and their castles are built on the tops of tall mountains. These men are called Kadji because they are banded together. Each is skilled beyond any other men in the arts of sorcery."

"From their hands, much harm is done to men, though none can harm them. Those who go out to battle against the armies of Kadjeti are blinded by some strange magic. Sorcerers call forth winds or send them away. They call down storms from clear skies and dash the ships of their attackers upon the rocks."

"They can also run across the water as though on dry land. Or should they choose, they can turn night into day, brightening the darkest places as though a sun had come to earth. These are also reasons why we call them Kadjis, but they are human like us."

"They can be killed, though it is no easy task, for their magic protects them. Most often, it is only one Kadj who can kill another. Otherwise, there are no weapons mortal men possess that can easily harm them. I hope you recall the story of how I found the maiden. Do you remember when I told you two of my Kadji servants were slain?"

"To engage them in battle is not for the faint of heart. Those who fought that day were all Kadj. No one knows why or how they can kill each other but cannot be harmed by others. Many have speculated on this, but no one has ever found the answer."

Avtandil was pleased to hear what she said. In only a few words, she gave him news armies might have died on the fields to learn. He thanked her profusely, praising her and God in the same breath.

"Your words have extinguished the fires of concern which burned me for the maiden you spoke of. I am greatly pleased to hear the evil of Kadji is born of men and not purely supernatural. If they can kill each other, then there exists a way for others to kill them. Perhaps some hope yet exists for her. Do not despair yet."

"Instead, praise God. Thank Him, for it is his divine providence that brought us together. He is the unheard comforter of our hearts, washing away every woe. The Unspeakable One, who was and is forever merciful. See how His light spreads over us now?"

Phatman thought the praise Avtandil gave was for her. Desire burned once more in her for the Knight, but he kept his secret. He did not share his heart's truth with her, nor his love for another. Instead, he gave himself over to loving her, as she wished.

She embraced his neck, nestling her face into it before wrapping herself around him. Together they pulled the clothes from one another, fabric falling in a heap before man and woman once more became one.

They shook one another, intertwined fingers grasping at the warmth and intimacy lovers share. Skin caressed skin, and their hearts beat in time to the breath shared between their lips. But Avtandil shook with more than passion.

Though Phatman enjoyed lying with him, a secret regret gripped the Knight. But he did not resist her caresses. And when she climbed on him again, he embraced her neck, becoming one with her until they lay spent and exhausted.

Unbeknownst to his lover, remembrance of Tinatin seared Avtandil's soul. It maddened his heart, leaving it racing within his chest like a steed before a storm. He thought himself a fool, trading the rose he held for a foreign blossom.

He'd heard sages say how crows who find roses think themselves to be nightingales. Yet he, already nightingale, had traded roses for lilies. In doing so, he betrayed his own rose and became a crow.

CHAPTER 14 –

THE MERCHANT'S DECEPTION

When the sun rose on Avtandil the following day, its rays were unkind to him. He was soiled by what he had done that night and did again in the morning. He went to bathe, and Phatman gave him whatever he wanted to wear. She still believed him to be a merchant and dressed him as such.

Though, for his part, he was tired of playing the role of a fool. He said as much to her.

"Today, I will show you the truth of my affairs. You will see me as I am and not as you have seen these many days we have spent together. Tonight, I will return to you in my own manner of dress. Then the thread of my own tale will be revealed to you."

She smiled at him, thinking he had some particularly fanciful clothes he would return with. However, she loved him as he was, regardless of whatever he might wear. With promises to return in the evening, he left. For a time, she also rested. But as the day grew long, she began preparing a meal for him. It was the custom of her people to cook for a man they loved or respected. She wanted to show him this honor and busied herself with that task.

Meanwhile, he returned to the merchants' ship and told them his charade was finished. From this day, he would dress as himself and no longer wear the robes and garb of a merchant. Instead, he would appear as the Knight he was.

He put on his clothes and bound his boots, carefully lacing the leather straps. From there, he strapped on the curved sword he customarily wore. Satisfied with his appearance, he returned to Phatman's home.

When she saw the Knight appareled in his proper form, her breath caught in her throat. Words escaped her, for his beauty had increased beyond measure. Now the lion more closely resembled the sun than any merchant ever had. She invited him in, and everyone who saw him swooned at his appearance.

He laughed, seeing how many there failed to recognize him as the merchant he had been in the morning. Those who were mad with desire for him before wholly lost their hearts when they laid eyes on him in the garb of a Knight. He thought Phatman also didn't honestly believe it was he who stood before her and laughed out loud at the idea.

Like a young horse, he pranced and played, free from the confines of behaving like a merchant. They ate and drank together, and though he took some liberties with her in their private moments, he did not go further. Instead, they shared their time more like dear and affectionate friends than lovers.

They talked late into the evening, and then the Knight returned home. He lay down in his bed with joy at returning to himself after so long in disguise. His sleep was deep and pleasant, lasting until evening. On waking, he took a messenger with him and walked high up into the gardens of Gulansharo to a private place. Then he sent the man to invite Phatman to him, telling her to come, as he was very much alone and desired her company.

When she arrived, her heart was once more lost at the sight of him. And as she greeted him, he heard the whisper of their shared intimacies hidden in the soft tones of her voice. He remembered their time together. His heart began to beat more quickly, and her eyes pierced his soul when she spoke.

"How is it I am more slain by the sight of you with each new meeting? Your form is like that of a spruce tree. Meanwhile, the timbre of your voice ignites a fire in the deepest places of my body. What man has ever existed who I might compare you to?"

He smiled at her praise of him and wrapped her in a powerful embrace. Then, he beckoned toward the carpet and pillows he had arranged on the ground. They sat together, with the sun setting between them. Its light cast shadows from the eaves of their eyelashes, adding shade to the rose gardens of their cheeks. Avtandil took her hands in his, and looking into her eyes, he began to speak.

"You are dear to me, Phatman. A good and trustworthy friend without an equal. Yet, I fear what I tell you now will leave you trembling as though you have been bitten by a serpent. You have yet to hear the truth of who I am or where my heart rests. You believe I am a merchant and master of a caravan, but this is not true."

CHAPTER 15 –

A CURE FOR SORROW

"I command the armies of Arabia under the wise and mighty King Rostevan. He is the Lord of our hosts, but I answer only to him and one other. In my hands are countless treasuries and the entirety of our Kingdom's military arsenal."

"Of that one other who commands me, it is his only child and daughter, Tinatin. She is a sun and enlightens the lands. It is her who consumes me. I am slain by her lashes of black, formed like trees. Her order is what brought me to you. In service to her, I forsook the orders of my King and left in search of a man none could find."

"First, I sought him. For three years, I traveled over the world seeking the Knight in the Panther Skin until I found him. His name is Tariel, the last Prince of India. And in his name, I left to seek out the woman he loves. She who drives him mad. Whom the loss of has left his soul bitter and wasted. Once proud, he lies now like a wounded and pale lion, empty of heart and strength to do more than wait for my return."

Then, Avtandil shared the entirety of his story with Phatman. They sat together under the stars, sipping wine and eating bits of this and that as he related the tale. First, he told of meeting Asmath in the cave of the Devi and then Tariel. After this, he spoke of returning to Arabia. Then he explained how he left in the night like a thief to return to the caves.

Finally, he spoke of finding a broken and battered Tariel between the corpses of a lion and a panther. Though the memory pained him, he described how his friend had one foot in this world and the other in the next. He went on about meeting Phridon and ended with his time on the seas until arriving in Gulansharo. There, he met Phatman and, by chance, came to rescue her from Kurva while learning of the mysterious maiden.

She listened in wonder, sometimes exclaiming over this or that, or asking for more detail. She knew many places Avtandil spoke of, but others were a mystery. Though above all, she wanted to hear of the maiden. When he finished the story, he directly addressed the story of Nestan with her.

"Phatman, though you do not know it, you are the balm of he whom you have not met. This man Tariel, whom I spoke of. His eyelashes are like the ruffled wings of a raven, and he is of even greater constitution than I. Of the woman he loves, who you also are equally bound to, her name is Nestan Daredjan."

"I think, if we work together, you and I can be of use to them. Those two stars can be reunited, and all the world will shine brighter for the good deed we have done. Between us both, we can find some way for these lovers to meet again."

"Summon your sorcerer, the same one who led me to

the home of Kurva and witnessed the deed from afar. You told me before how he went to Kadjeti Castle and returned with news of Nestan. So, he must have some means to travel there and back again."

"You can compose a letter for the maiden. Tell her of all you have seen and all which has come to pass. Doubtless, she will be mad with loneliness and desperate with grief over what Fate has done to her. Be soft in your words but be sure she also tells us the truth of where she is and what is there."

"Ask her what she wants, and whatever she chooses, we will respect and abide by her decision. When she answers, we can decide what course of action best suits the task of liberating her. God may yet grant that you hear tidings of the ruin of Kadjeti and all therein. With our combined might, we may be able to remove the stain of this evil from the world."

Phatman agreed with what the Knight said and hastily summoned one of the Kadj sorcerers who served her. She touched the amulet around her neck, and in a moment, the man was standing before her. He bowed before turning and smiling at Avtandil. Then he asked how he might be of service to his lady. She answered, and from her words, their course was decided.

"The glory of what I ask of you now belongs to God. You cannot believe what I have heard this day. My years are lengthened into the edged of eternity from these tidings. I must send you back to Kadjeti, though your journey will be long."

"Prepare yourself in the next hours; I will give you a letter to deliver to the maiden you once saved from those Kadj slavers. You must take it to her in the highest tower of Kadjeti Castle, where she is held. Allow her time to give an answer and return to me with it."

"In doing so, you will quench the furnace of fires

burning within me. With the news you bring, we may find a cure for the maiden's sorrow and reunite her with the one she loves. Can you do this for me?"

The sorcerer bowed and smiled once more before speaking.

"What the Lady wishes shall be done. I will depart this evening with your letter and deliver it to the maiden. As you have expressed the urgency of this task, no more than an evening or three shall pass before my return. When your letter is composed, call to me, and I will take it into Kadjeti."

CHAPTER 16 –

MESSAGES AND MISSIVES

Avtandil and Phatman returned to her home. Once there, the lady began writing a letter to Nestan. Her hand shook as she wrote, for until learning of Tariel, she had lost all hope of rescuing the maiden from her Fate. Now, there was a glimmer of hope. Her words were as follows.

"My star and Heavenly sun, the light of those consumed with grief by your absence. You who are lovely as crystal and ruby mingled together. I am writing to you about things I have heard and learned in your absence. Though the learning of them has not brought me joy."

"Yet, as is often the case with the truth of a thing, it has comforted my heart. May what I write now bring you happiness, for I write of Tariel, who endlessly searches for you. He has been maddened by grief these many years and, until now, had no news of you."

"His sworn brother is an Arabian Knight named

Avtandil. He came to Gulansharo on a quest to learn news of you or your whereabouts, and Fate brought him to me. This Hero seeks information concerning the fortress of Kadjeti and the Witch Queen."

"Has she returned home with her sorcerers yet? Do you know the number of warriors left behind to guard the castle? Have you seen who their Chief is or what race he may be?"

"Whatever you know concerning these things, please share it with us. I know Avtandil to be a trustworthy and honest man. With his help, once more, you could be united with Tariel. I beg you, write to me and tell us of these things!"

"We will await your decision and work to do whatever you desire. This is why I have sent my servant, who once rescued you from your captors. Whatever news you send it back with, please give us some token for Tariel too. Avtandil will return to him with it and share your wishes and desires. May it please God to grant me the joy of helping to reunite you and your lover, who both are fitted to be among the Lights of Heaven."

She finished her letter and let Avtandil read over it. They agreed it was enough, and so it would be sent. Phatman sealed it with wax and a gold threaded ribbon, dripping a bit of her perfume onto the paper as she did so. Then she turned to the sorcerer and bade him deliver it to the maiden.

"Give this letter directly into the hands of she who bears eyes of jet and a face of crystal and sunlit ruby. Hasten in your journey and be swift of knee. I envy your path, for it will bring you to her who consumes my heart. She will look on you, and more, her hands will be upon this parchment."

"Have no small pity for me, but do not let it lengthen your steps. Move with grace and speed and be wary of

Witch Queen's cunning. I would not have her know any measure of our intent or your comings and goings."

The sorcerer took the rolled and sealed letter in his hands, carefully examining it before tucking it into his robes. Then, he smiled, white teeth flashing from his ebony face, before bowing and turning away from Phatman and Avtandil. Wrapping a shimmering green cape around himself, he stepped from the edge of the balcony and vanished.

Like an arrow shot into the night from the bow of Artemis, he flew across the city's rooftops. Though Kadjeti was far, he arrived just as the sun was setting. Mingling with the gray of twilight and wrapping shadow about himself, he strode past the Knights guarding the outer gates. His steps carried him deep into the fortress of Kadjeti, and before long, he made his way to the tower where Nestan was kept.

CHAPTER 17 –

SECRETS OF THE SORCERERS

He paused and, and with a wave of his hands, passed through the closed gates to the tower as if they had stood open. None saw him as he ascended the tower stairs. When he arrived in the outer chambers of the maiden's prison, he made a sound appear from the other side of the room. It drew away the eunuch's attention, and the sorcerer passed through the door to her room as if it were a curtain instead of iron and wood.

Once in the room with that sun, he appeared, cloaked in his robes. Long dark hair framed his smiling face, but Nestan drew back in fear. The color of her cheeks changed from rose and saffron to the violet and blue of an evening sky.

Concern and fear etched her face. She believed the man to be an assassin or worse. Maybe he came to hurt or kidnap her to a darker fate than the one she now suffered. But the sorcerer did not know this.

Ever smiling, he held out the rolled and perfumed parchment, looking at Nestan expectantly. But she hesitated, keeping her distance. She was not reassured of his intentions, so he spoke.

"Dear maiden, who am I for you to fear? Do you not remember me, who rescued you from captivity once before at the edges of the sea? I am Phatman's sworn servant, and this letter is written by her hand. She bade me deliver it to you."

"I assure you, there is no falsehood in what I say. On these pages, you will find justification for my arrival and news of another sort. Open the rose of your heart to what I hold, and you will see it bears you no harm. Do not fear me, nor fade so quickly. Let the sun of your presence be revealed from behind the clouds of your fright."

At first timid, but then with a boldness born of curiosity and remembered trust in the sorcerer who once saved her, she stepped forward. With trembling hands, she untied the letter and rolled out the pages. Hot tears fell from the almond and jet of her eyes as she read what was written therein.

When she finished, a light shone from her eyes. She breathed a heavy and deep sigh. Looking up at the man, she asked what he knew of the person who sought her and how anyone understood she was still alive.

He smiled once more, not unlike a wise man looking on the face of a child. Reaching out, he plucked the letter from her hands and returned it to the depths of his robes. Then he spoke, enlightening the maiden.

"Little bird, men like me do not deal in things that are not absolute. It is the source of our power to fully measure the certainty in all things. So, I can only tell you what I know without speculation or coloration of fact."

"When you left upon the steed Phatman gave you, the sun of our house grew dark. It was as if lances pierced every part of Phatman's being. Your loss left her too weak to remove the barbs from her soul. Because of this, she could do no more than suffer their weight. None of us could aid her nor stop the sea from filling with the sorrow she was consumed by."

"However, there came a day when some travelers entered the city. One man amongst them shared the story of a light in the dark, captured by an evil man from Kadjeti. Phatman knew it to be you and sent me to confirm your whereabouts. Her sorrow increased when she understood the ill Fate had laid upon you. Since that time, she has been nearly inconsolable."

"Yet a man came to us from afar. A Knight of Arabia, fair of face. He is formed like a spruce tree from the Garden of Eden. His arms are thick like those of a Hero. She told him all that had happened to you since your rescue from the slavers."

"In time, we learned you were the reason he came to Gulansharo. His sworn brother is your own Tariel. So, Avtandil and Phatman sent me to you. I was instructed to come here with haste and secrecy, delivering the words you have just read. As you have learned from her letter, I must also return with news of you and whatever you know of this place."

Joy lit her face as he spoke, for she knew his words to be true. None could have known all he told and what had been written in the letter. Somehow the providence of Heaven had seen fit to shine a light into her darkness. Beyond any dream of hope or chance of redemption, she had found a glimmer of hope. To know Tariel remained living was a joy she could not contain.

She begged the sorcerer to wait as she composed two letters. The first to Phatman, and a second to Tariel. The man whom the sun of her heart rose and set on. Her Knight in the Panther Skin, the last Prince of India.

CHAPTER 18 -

PHATMAN'S REPRIEVE

Nestan glowed like a star as she wrote. Her joyous resolve brightened the room. The sorcerer stood silent, with his arms tucked into his sleeves. He watched as she wrote, taking note of each word.

"With this letter, you shall know how my heart boils and aches with desire unrealized. These many years I did not dare to dream of my freedom. Yet your words give wings to my hope once more. You light my face with the sun, igniting fires in my heart I thought long since dead."

"You are a mother to me. Nay, better than a mother! For all my days, it seems Fate bears an ill will towards me. Grief has always been added to my griefs, and sorrow draped about me like a funeral garb. But with your letter, I perceive the dawn may not be far removed from my sight. I thank you for this and more."

"It was your hand which saved me from those two Kadj brutes and my torment in their magical chest. You alleviated a portion of the woe I carried in that gesture alone. Now, held as I am by the force of an entire Kingdom, your gentle hand reaches into my darkness. Your light guides me, and a thousand Heavens might never fully return the kindness you have shown me."

"But I must tell you where I am and how they hold me. Around my tower alone, there are many thousands of Heroes. I can see them from the windows when I look down through the bars. Yet more still occupy other areas. Though I cannot accurately measure their numbers, their might is equal to what I have seen of the armies of India or Persia."

"It will be no small thing for several of the greatest hosts of soldiers in the world to reach me. But with one or two men, even were they supported by all the armies of India, it is not possible. Believe me, there is no hope of any quest to free me from these chains. My Fate is sealed without an army."

"Though, as you have asked, I will tell too of the Dulardukht, Witch Queen of Kadjeti. She has not long since left. Perhaps the space of less than one moon. With certainty, she will be gone a year or more. They go to the far north, across Persia, to the fortress of Alamut, though I cannot say where it is. I only heard talk of where they would go and the difficulty of such a journey."

"But these things do not matter. Of what concern can they be? Whoever seeks me cannot succeed. Let them not be consumed with the fire of any hope for my salvation. There is no possibility, but I envy them, for they see the sun and taste freedom. Yet, it brings me joy to know my Tariel still lives and breathes. Though my life may be piteous without him to carry my burden, I will endure."

"As I write this to you, it comes to my mind that I have not yet told of my woe. Nor did I share any measure of the tragedies which consumed me and darkened my days. I hid these things from you, though not with intent. My tongue was unable to give voice to what boiled within my soul. The torment was so great I could find no words."

"But I beg of you, spare me further pain. Do not let my beloved seek to find or rescue me. Let him have pity on me, lest my Fate be worsened. I bear enough hurt to give some to every living thing and still die from my pain. Should he come to this place and force me to look on him as a corpse, I will suffer woe greater than I can carry. I would die a double death."

"There are none who can help me. Be as certain of this as I am and accept what Fate has decreed. Tariel will break himself against these walls if he does not listen to you. And I will be stoned with granite and buried forever in my misery. Whatever you must do, convince him not to come."

"Of a token, I shall cut a piece from the veils he gave me. I will give it to your sorcerer, wrapped in a letter I will write to Tariel. You know how I cling to these veils, though they are black like my Fate. This is because they remind me of him and forever will."

When she finished writing, she waited for the ink to dry and carefully folded the paper. Putting it off to the side, she began composing a message for Tariel.

CHAPTER 19 –

FOR THE MEMORY OF LOVE

With fire in her eyes and tears drooping the raven tailfeathers of her eyelashes, Nestan began to write to Tariel. She reflected on the brevity of the time they shared together and smiled. The rose of her lips opened, revealing the pearl of her teeth. Her thoughts were of the man she loved, whose tears could quench the hottest of her fires.

"You, who cause the willow to bend and weep at the river's edge. How might my hands address that which my tongue has never fully composed? Perchance these words I craft must be formed of more than the stuff of poets and philosophers. Let me use my own form as a pen, and for paper, take my heart glued to yours forever. Of ink, I will dip into the black well of sorrow which drowns us both. From there, I pray the truth of these words will shine evermore upon your steps."

"Until this day, I believed you had been slain. Never

did I think to escape those who held me, for what benefit might it have earned me? I thought you, who I love above all else in the world, had perished. To me, the blood of my life had fled. No resource remained to me which had not turned to ash, and so I closed myself to the world."

"Now, my heart soars as I hear of your life and liberty. I bow before God and thank Him for this news of you. Whatever grief I carried before will be measured as joy from this day forward. Your life is enough for me to carry hope in my soul. But let me tell you a little about what has happened recently. If I were to tell you about these things in their entirety, I would grow old from the length of telling it."

"Those evil Kadj brutes who kidnapped me from India took me farther than I can say. We sailed on a glowing ship, like a pearl with sails of gossamer webs. They kept me in and out of a large chest, though my prison seemed to have some magic. I was neither hungry nor tired when locked therein. Neither did I sleep or dream. Only when they opened it did I have any awareness of the world or faculty of my mind."

"They came to this far and distant place called Gulansharo, the city of flowers. On the shores of this sea, Lady Phatman saw my plight and rescued me at no small cost to herself. May God forever protect her. But Fate was not content to see me free. Instead, fresh brands were laid upon my soul."

"Now I am held prisoner and locked behind the might of an army of Kadjis and their slaves. The likes of which I have seen no equal. They hold me against my will in a tower so high my eyes can barely see the ground beneath. There are gates of adamant and more portcullises than I can count between here and my freedom."

"Beyond where I am, there lies a tunnel longer than an archer's shot. Day and night, the sentries patrol it, numbering in the tens of thousands. Sword and spear are complimented by bows and massive siege weapons. Whoever may come to this place will surely be overcome by them like fire consuming parchment."

"No doubt you will think to rescue me, as you have forever been my Hero. But I must beg you not to consider this. Do not slay me with the addition of woe to that which already burdens me. If I were to see you dead, it would burn me to ash like tinder struck by flint and steel."

"You must accept that the evil hand of Fate has sundered us forever, so long as we occupy this earth. No power can reunite us, so I must ask you to renounce me. Harden your heart more than stone, and do not deepen the furrow of your sorrow with additional grief."

CHAPTER 20 –

ALL WE HAVE IS LOST

"**M**ake no mistake. There is no other for me than you. I will never forget the light of your eyes or the strength of your form as you wrapped your arms around me. But I will console myself with the knowledge you live, and so will continue my life. Should you perish, I would slay myself with a dagger or find some way to cast myself from this tower and onto the rocks beneath."

"My love will never belong to any other than you. I am to you as the earth, and you are my moon. There can be only one. Though triple suns might shine, there would still be only one source of moonlight. Know this and accept the eternal commitment of my soul. Perhaps we will meet again when our time in this world has passed."

"I hope you will often think of me, for I will forever nurse the love we shared. But you must carry no more than thoughts of me in remembrance. Do not harbor anger or resentment towards Fate or these Kadjis who hold me, for I am lost to you. There is no way by which you might make your way here and still live to see me."

"Instead, look at me and remember what deeds the world does. Fashion yourself the armor of wisdom from this knowledge, for the wise know the world well. Therefore, it is contemptible to them, and they despise it. I, too, am like this. My life without you exists in darkness, however much light may shine on me."

"Give up your love and send it to Heaven with prayers for me. You know too well how time and Fate have cursed and abused us. No longer do we look to one another with joy. Instead, our hearts are rent by what we must do without one another. Perhaps in the secret places of your mind, what is hidden will manifest itself, and you will understand the truths I write."

"If you cannot harden your heart, turn your prayers to God. Only the power of Heaven could give us wings so that we might fly together once more. In this way, we might be delivered from the world's troubles and away from the elements. Together we could spend day and night looking down on the sun and moon for all eternity."

"Your voice alone might be heard, for even the sun cannot endure without you. You are made of it, and every atom of your being is a part, no different than the sign of Leo in the sky. In fact, as I write this, I am reminded that whenever I look to the Heavens, I will be reminded of you. You will shine on me whether by the sun or stars and moon."

"Take pity on me and forgive the length of my speech. These are the last words I will write to you. If life was bitter to me, may I look forward to the sweetness of death and a return to your embrace. To die, I realize, is no longer a grievous thing. My soul is committed to you, and I have made a bed for my heart made from your love. Though our parting adds wounds to my soul, I would not have you weep and mourn the loss of me."

"Instead, return to India. Help my father, for no doubt he is surrounded by enemies and helpless on all sides without you. Command our armies, and do not let our beloved home fall to invaders. Together you and my father may comfort one another. No doubt he also suffers the pain of separation from me."

"Any complaints I have voiced against my Fate are sufficient. There is no more for me to say of it. True justice goes from one heart to another. This is the way of lovers. One day I will die and become food for the ravens. But until that time, I will weep and suffer enough for us both. Go on and live your life."

"All of the Seven Heavens turned the wheel of their wrath against us for what we did. However, from this day, our fates must be unchained. You are free. I will carry your burden. Take this strip of cloth, cut from the veils you gave me. It is a token of the truth of what I have written herein. I will keep the rest of this strange cloth with me, for it reminds me of all the hopes and dreams we once held together."

With tears at the edges of her eyes and a trembling hand, Nestan removed her veils. Then, with a strange knife from the sorcerer, she cut a small strip from their end. She folded this cloth into the letter she had written Tariel and set it to the side. Bareheaded, the wind stirred her hair, which had grown long in the years she had been lost. Aloe scent wafted from her, drifting away on the night air like a raven on the wing.

CHAPTER 21 –

THE PRINCE'S DECISION

The sorcerer took the letters and his knife, bowing to her as he turned to leave. Once more, he wrapped the strange glimmering green cloth around himself and disappeared. Distant winds from the northern deserts of Arabia carried south to Gulansharo.

Fate brought the humble servant home to his master. None therein knew how important the matter of Nestan and Tariel was to him. Nor did he speak of it. Instead, he held to the promise of an end to one thing and the beginning of another.

Phatman and Avtandil were seated next to each other on an unlit balcony beneath the stars when he arrived. He smiled at the sight of them, white teeth glistening in the moonlight. Knight and lady thanked God for the servant's speedy and safe return, eager to hear what he had to say about Nestan and Kadjeti fortress.

"Lady Phatman, I have done as you asked and delivered

your letters to the one held prisoner in the tower of Kadjeti Castle. She gave me two letters. One is for you, and the other to the man who holds her heart, Tariel, the last Prince of India. I give them to you and will return to my affairs if you no longer require my services."

Once the sorcerer left, Phatman opened the letters and read them. She shed no small number of tears at what Nestan wrote to her. In part for the thanks she gave, but more because of the tragedy she hadn't known the maiden suffered. However, when she read the letter to Tariel, her concern grew, which she shared with Avtandil.

"My lion, these words will do no more than stoke the fire of the man she loves! He will become maddened by what is written here and surely make an assault on Kadjeti. Yet should the Kadjis return before you arrive, there is clearly no road you might take which would not end in ruin."

"If you do not accompany him, he will die alone. But if you go together, both of you will perish. All the light remaining in my life will be extinguished. I will be left to dwell forever in darkness until the end of my days!"

Avtandil thought about what she said and knew it to be true. In no way would he abandon Tariel or the deed before them. However, wisdom is often sharper than any blade. He did not fear slaves and soldiers, but lacking weapons they might use against any Kadj men who might be there could prove troublesome. He did not want the blood of his friend on his hands. Nor did he desire to bring an army to entertain what would undoubtedly end in death for them.

Unsure of any course other than his need to return to Tariel with Nestan's letter, he shared his thoughts with Phatman.

"Ever winding and never-ending are the roads of Heroes. Though I could not have known I might meet you or learn the Fate of this maiden, here I stand. What I wished to find when I left Tariel has been found. However, my time grows short. I must return to him and do not have the leisure to tarry here."

"But you must know I have no thoughts of abandoning my brother. I will do whatever must be done to aid my brother. However, I did not travel so far alone. There are many armies to be had between myself and those Heroes you have yet to meet."

"We do not fear to rally against the evil of Kadjeti. Additionally, it is the work of men and Knights like us to do things like this. If we are swift with our return, I can lead Tariel to the home of the Witch Queen before she returns to her cauldron. And then their fortress will fall."

Then he called for the men Phridon had sent with him. Those four brave Knights were not slow in coming. They listened intently to what he said.

"Men of Mulghazanzar. I have called you to me with news of our quest. Though we have been no more or less active than corpses until this day, life is returned to us, for we have learned of what we sought. The maiden we have all been looking for is found!"

"However, she is held captive by a fierce and unyielding enemy. Our time is short, for we cannot overcome them by force of arms alone. We must use cunning and turn their weapon of choice against them. This thing they fight with is deceit, which they are masters of. We will leave them stricken with woe and crippled by fear if we succeed."

"Now I must ask you to return alone to Phridon. I cannot attend him now, for my time is short. There are only a few weeks left on the road I must travel. Let him strengthen his armies and choose men to join our cause. I will return to him in one month or at most three. From there, we will make our way to the fortress of our enemy."

"I will give every detail to him in a letter, which I must ask you to deliver. This service is of utmost importance, but the burden laid upon me with your accomplishment of what I have requested is greater. To compensate you for this task, I place into your hands what is left to me of the treasures we liberated from the pirates."

"Though I would give you more, my home is not near. It is not within my power to dispense gifts worthy of your service. Instead, I must command you to prepare yourselves."

Phatman will give you a fast ship with which you must make haste. But first, you must wait for me to finish composing the letter I would have you give Phridon."

CHAPTER 22 -

A LETTER BETWEEN FRIENDS

With no small measure of excitement, Avtandil sat to compose his letter. Though he had not been idle, he felt his hands had worked more towards opaque ends than the clarity he was accustomed to dealing with as a Knight. This letter was a boon to his spirit.

Tariel, Last Prince of India and the Knight in the Panther Skin, was no ordinary man. But to Avtandil, he was, first and foremost, a brother. He would do everything in his power to reunite his friend with Nestan and restore him to his rightful place on the throne. With these thoughts in his mind, he began to write.

"Phridon, brother, and Lord of Mulghazanzar, I come to you with what we hoped to learn. Nestan has been found! By the grace of God and no small amount of chance, we found the city of Gulansharo. Therein I met Lady Phatman, a lady who is the wife of Usen, Lord of the merchant houses. Though not everything went as planned, I received compensation for the pains I suffered in the form of news."

"I have the truth of what happened to Nestan, she who has a face which lights the world like a sun. Now I must return to the lion Tariel. Undoubtedly, the knowledge his beloved has been found will renew his spirit. He was near death when I left and close to the earth. But all doubt and shadow will be cast from his mind when he hears this."

"However, Nestan is not free. Dulardukht, the Witch Queen of Kadjeti, has captured her. She is held in the castle's highest tower and guarded by countless host of Knights and soldiers. But, with the aid of Tariel, we three and those we command can overcome their defenses, though it will entail a fierce battle."

"But we may only succeed if we do not delay. The Queen has left to mourn her sister's death in the far northern fortress of Alamut. She has taken all the sorcerers and best Knights of Kadjeti with her. They will be gone for one year, though a month or more has already passed."

"If I were to go alone, perhaps I would end ruined and broken. My Fate would be no more than any other corpse littering the fields of Kadjeti. But I am sure the most difficult roads will be easy if you and our brother Tariel go with me. None can stand against you, and whatever your desire is made yours. One who threw a stone at you would see it soften before it fell!"

"But my words grow long. Without their magics, those who guard Kadjeti are only men. Meanwhile, these hands tire of pens and paper, longing instead for swords and battle. I am sorry I do not have the leisure to deliver this message myself, but our time goes short. I must go in the other direction and travel with haste. Little time remains to us if we are to rescue that moon from captivity."

"I will not be long in coming to you with Tariel. Expect

us in one month, or at most three. Though our purpose may be grim, we will come with joy and merriment. Rejoice when you see us. What more can I say than this? The men you sent with me have served admirably and with honor. It is they who bring this letter to you. May you find joy in this knowledge, for every like gives birth to like."

Satisfied with his message, Avtandil rolled and tied the letter. He gave it to the men of Phridon, again confirming he had told them all they needed to know. Then he sent them on their way, ensuring they understood their task's urgency and message. They confirmed what he said, saluted, and went to the ship Phatman had arranged.

As the ship passed from sight and disappeared into the night sea, Avtandil turned to Phatman. She knew he must go but begged him to stay until mid-morning. That way, she could spend some last few moments with him, and he would be able to leave with the tide. That night they dined together. His heart was heavy, knowing he would leave the woman he had spent all his time in Gulansharo with.

In the morning, he left, taking his horse, and boarding a fast ship that would take him north up the coast of Africa. Phatman's heart was filled with woe at his going, but she knew he could not stay. What time they shared was a thing she would forever cherish, and she hoped to see him again. Still, his departure left her feeling as though her joy had been buried.

CHAPTER 23 –

HEARTBREAK AND HUMILITY

The ship Avtandil sailed with made good time. It crossed the seas without mishap, and he was glad to be alone with his thoughts during the voyage. Lifting his hands, he thanked God and placed hope in Him for what the future might hold. Soon he would arrive at a place no more than a week or two from the caves of the Devi. Soon, he would see Tariel and Asmath and give them the good news of his success.

As his ship drew near the port, he saw the lands were blossoming with life. Everything was green. This was a sign the roses outside the caves were soon to bloom.

When the ship docked, he left with his horse and gear. Riding out of the small town and down a verdant path, he recognized small flowers and greens native to the lands where he had spent so much time. Though the sky was overcast, his heart leaped at the knowledge that he would soon meet his sworn brother and sister. Whatever storms might come were of little concern to him.

Rain was a constant to those who traveled. In the last

four years, he had worn more roads than most men in a lifetime. Because of this, he was no stranger to the weather, and when the rain finally started, he lifted his arms over his head.

The sky thundered, and crystal droplets fell through his upturned hands. They kissed the rose of his lips, and he rejoiced in the storm's glory, likening it to a message from Tinatin. Without her beside him, he spoke to the sky, singing praises and laughing as the downpour soaked him and his horse.

He traveled across deserted and pathless tracks for almost a week through regions unknown to any man. Wherever he encountered lions or panthers stalking him, he slew them until he saw the rocky outcropping which marked the entrance to the caves of the Devi. When he drew near, he saw the caves but wondered if his brother would be there.

He knew his friend would not linger in the stone halls of the cave, so he decided to look in the fields. After all, Tariel was given to roam like a beast. He was restless in the absence of Nestan or any ability to aid her. Thinking this, Avtandil picked up his pace and rode in a wide arc across the plains.

The Hero shouted and sang as he went, gaily calling out to his friend in a cheerful voice between verses of random and silly songs. Before long, he came to the edge of the rushes. There stood his brother, shining like the sun on a cloudless day. He stood over the corpse of a slain lion, blood dripping from his sword.

Tariel looked up, hearing the shouts and songs of Avtandil. He dropped his sword at the sight of his friend, letting out a great cry and bounding towards him like a child running to a lost parent. Avtandil did the same, nearly falling from his horse in the process, and the two met in a fierce and brotherly embrace.

The two brothers looked at one another, unable to believe they were together again after so long apart. Tariel spoke first, telling his friend how he had worked daily on his body and mind. He clung to the hope of good news and strengthened himself and his resolve. This was why he had been out battling lions.

Avtandil laughed when he heard this from his friend. Then he put a hand on Tariel's shoulder, looking him in the eyes as he spoke.

"Brother, lions are no match for your skill. But I have found a worthy enemy where you may test your blade earnestly. The tidings I bring are of the best sort, for they will renew the flower of your soul. Those roses that grow outside the Devi caves will wilt with envy, for your rose will bloom as it never has."

Tariel brushed aside Avtandil's hand, laughing at how serious he had become.

"Today, I have enough joy for a hundred more years. You have returned, and in seeing you, I have realized all I desired this last year. Whatever else I might want, God may or may not give. What can I do to change one thing or another?"

"No man can find anything in this world that Heaven does not ordain. Let us rejoice, and do not be so serious. There is enough time tomorrow for whatever you would say to me. For now, let us go and see Asmath. She has missed you almost as much as I did."

Slowly, Avtandil realized his friend did not understand the truth he carried. So, he reached into his pack and removed the letter Nestan had written. He handed it to Tariel, who looked at the parchment in confusion. Then, the Indian opened it and saw the fringe of cloth she had cut from her veils. He lifted the paper and fabric together, touching and pressing them to his face.

Then, with the suddenness of a lightning strike, his

rosy cheeks went pale as winter snow. Gasping as his heart faltered, he collapsed like a stone. His jet hair waved like a torn flag as the ground rushed up to embrace his lifeless form.

CHAPTER 24 –

THE LOSS OF TARIEL

Avtandil was too late. The sorrows Tariel carried were so great neither Cain nor Solomon could have endured them, and now he lay lifeless and empty as a harp without strings. Consumed with worry, Avtandil rushed to the side of his fallen companion.

Afraid his actions might have forever dimmed the lights of Tariel's eyes, he labored to return his friend to life. In those fleeting moments, the world stood still, but his best efforts produced no results. Frustrated, he began berating himself for his stupidity.

"How could I be such a fool? The ruby of my heart breaks at what I have done to my friend. No madman or fool would have done as I have, and now my hands disgrace me. In my haste, I poured water on fires of oil and so spread the flames. I should have known a heart so stricken as Tariel's cannot bear such joy as my hasty actions laid upon him."

"I have been a fool, and stupid men cannot do well for themselves or anyone else in difficult matters. Had I thought for even a moment, the words I chose may have been more measured. My actions could have been less hasty. Indeed, it is better to be reprimanded for being slow than to receive praise for unnecessary haste."

But the words he spoke against himself did nothing to help the situation. At a loss for what else to do, he went to look for fresh water in the nearby rushes. His hope was to quench the flames consuming his friend and rouse him. However, there was none to be found. Yet the corpse of the freshly slain lion was there.

With no other options, Avtandil took blood from it and carried it back to Tariel. He tore open his friend's shirt and threw the blood on the man's face and chest. Bright red spots colored the lapis lazuli of his skin, leaving him looking like a bloodstone struck by Pan's hoof.

The blood of one lion mixed with that of another. Color began returning to Tariel as the power of Heaven breathed life back into him. His chest shuddered and heaved. Then he uttered a long and shaking sigh before opening his eyes and sitting up.

The sun's brightness dispelled the moon's shadow, which had cast blue light over his form. Confused, he looked first to the sky and then around him. Slowly, his heart began to find its steps, and the hosts of India once more marched through the veins of their last prince.

In anguish, he shouted his pain and suffering at the world. The cry echoed back from the reeds and plains, but there was no other answer. His loss was that of a nation wronged, but this was the way of life.

Winter causes every rose to fade. Their leaves and petals grow cold and lifeless until they fall back to the earth. Then, the sun's intensity burns them in summer, yet they suffer in silence.

Neither men nor Nightingales have any say in these matters, though they both complain. Some with songs and others with words. Still, nothing changes. Heat consumes, frost freezes, and the wounds of the living forever bleed. Yet the hearts of men and women were the hardest to deal with.

They were forever wounded. Maddened equally by grief and in joy but cursed by Fate to never be whole. Those who sought life had no choice but to trust the world, though it was eternally their foe.

But Tariel lived. He had not died. Though covered in the blood of a lion, he breathed. And then he sat, reaching for the letter, and bringing it to his face again. His eyes moved from one word to the next as they read what Nestan had written. Tears pooled in the corners of his eyes, and madness circled his mind like the darkness around a campfire.

Seeing the turmoil of his friend's thoughts, Avtandil stood and spoke sharply to him, snapping the Indian back to reality.

"What are these tears which pull at the corner of your eyes? This behavior is unworthy of an educated man, particularly one learned in the arts of war! Now is the time for smiles. We have what has until now eluded our grasp."

"Should our way not be to go now in quest of the sun? Do we not go now to her, who has been denied to you for so long? I, your sworn brother, and friend, know the way. It will be my joy to show you. Let us rejoice and make our way to Kadjeti.

We will let drawn swords be our guides and claim victory when our blades are sheathed in the bodies of the enemy. They will be reduced to carrion, and our path home will be untroubled. Tell me, is this not what you have so long sought and desired?"

On hearing the sharp words of his friend, Tariel looked

up. His eyes were lit with black and white lightning, glittering dangerously. He had been active in the year Avtandil was absent. His arms were bursting with muscle and sinew, and his legs were thick as tree trunks.

The color of his face was also renewed, and he shone like well-cut ruby. Like the sun, it seemed even the sky would turn towards the glory of his fullness. He reached up to Avtandil, who grasped his hand, and then he stood with a single motion. Embracing his brother, he gave the thanks his pain had caused him to forget.

"You, who are both friend and brother, cannot be praised enough for what you have done. May the wise forever speak of your service to me and the world. Like a spring flowing down from a high mountain, you have watered the barren plain of my heart. By your hand, flowers once more bloom there."

"Your actions have liberated me from the depths of misery. My eyes are now freed from the pools of sorrow I once bathed in. Though I wish to give thanks equal to the service you have done me, I would never see you or any other endure such pain."

"Instead, may God repay you in my stead. Let Him reward you from His place on high in the Heavens. I have no more or less than the sum of my life and that of India, which will forever be indebted to you."

With those words, the two embraced once more. Laughing like two youths before a ball game. They mounted their horses and rode to the caves of the Devi. Asmath waited there, no doubt expecting to only see Tariel. Though she did not know it yet, flowers would soon bloom in the garden of hope she kept.

CHAPTER 25 –

ANGEL OF THE MORNING SUN

When they rode up to the caves, Asmath came out. Her head was uncovered, as she only expected to see Tariel. But she was pleased to see Avtandil riding beside him on his white horse. But she could not understand why the two men were joyously singing.

Until then, she had never seen Tariel come to the caves with more than sorrow for a crown. Her mouth hung open in surprise, and she wondered at the miracle before her. Here stood the heart-torn and sorrowful prince of India, singing and laughing. She feared for his health, thinking he was perhaps drunk or had some injury of the mind.

Concern etched her face as she rushed to meet the two men. She did not know the news Avtandil brought with him. That which she had spent her every waking moment longing for. But the two men were not shy with the good tidings they brought. They smiled as she came, joyously shouting as she ran to meet them.

"Run to us and embrace the news we carry! Nestan has been found! The moon we have so long sought is within our grasp. What was hidden is now revealed. The grace of God shines upon us, and all will be illuminated in his light. Now the fires laid on our souls by Fate will be quenched, and all our sorrows turned into joy."

Avtandil jumped from his horse as he finished speaking, grabbing Asmath in a firm embrace. She shouted with joy at the news, tears coming unbidden to her. With a sob, she made a nest of his neck, burying her face as she clung to his form.

He was a rock on which she had found shelter from life's woes. A brother to mirror Tariel, but also an opposite, for his was the feather of hope to her. Fate had seen fit to make him a light in the darkness to cloak her sorrow these many years. And though he was both fierce and strong, his was a gentle touch.

The arms which now held her were nurturing and loving. She kissed Avtandil's neck and face, begging for details of the news he carried. And he was not shy of his words, telling her all.

"Sit and listen, oh angel of the morning sun. I will tell you all I have learned. But do not weep in the fields. Keep your tears from falling here before the caves you have so long known as a home."

"What words I have are nets for you to catch joy with. I tell you, fill your sails with what I will say. Then rest your tired heart in the arms of what we have accomplished."

With the patience of Job, Asmath let him speak, letting go of his hand as she listened. Avtandil told her of every moment, finishing with the last meeting between him and the sorcerers of Phatman. When he finished, Tariel handed her the letter from Nestan, speaking as he did.

"Herein rests the hand of her who has passed through

troubles we have not seen the like of. Look now at what she has written and see the cutting of her veils therein. Read her missive and let us put away the shadows that have darkened our skies until now. The sun now approaches."

With trembling hands, Asmath took the letter from his hands. She recognized the writing of her friend and mistress, to whom she had forever been devoted. Quaking like a woman possessed by a spirit, she slowly and carefully read the words.

Her demeanor changed from fear to wonder as understanding dawned on her, like dark clouds breaking open to reveal blue skies and bright sun. She laughed and cried at once as a rain of pent-up emotions washed away her sorrows. Again, she asked the two knights to confirm what she had read.

"Is it true? Do I read hope for us? Does the sun indeed shine again after such a long night?"

Avtandil put his hands on hers and reassured the maiden.

"What you have read is true. I witnessed many of these events with my own eyes, though I would not have believed the magic of those sorcerers had I not seen it for myself. Now, put your grief away."

"The sun shines upon us once more. God has seen fit to ease the ills which plagued us. We would do well to remember that the essence of good is everlasting, and His hand is on all things. There is no darkness which the bonds of friendship and love cannot overcome."

Asmath looked from Avtandil to Tariel. Surprise and awe were written across her face. She could barely believe what news the men brought. It was as though they caught stars from Heaven and handed them to her. She wept with joy at the impossibility of their accomplishment. Although Fate's cruelty had caused her to believe divine providence was no more than legend, now she witnessed the truth.

In the light of God's grace, she understood He would never forsake anyone who accepted Him. Thankful for His forgiveness and understanding, she took the Knights by the hand. Then she led them into the caves of the Devi. Once inside, they praised the Heavens again.

All three of them now understood God would never allow a fate so terrible as that which they believed themselves to have received. Each of them was at once shamed and thankful for the patience and understanding they now realized He on High had shown. Truly His love knew no bounds and had no end.

Then they sat together, discussing how best to rescue Nestan. It was certain they would need an army to lay siege to Kadjeti Castle and perhaps more than just an army. They knew Phridon would lend aid and men towards their cause, but his help would not be enough.

CHAPTER 26 –

INTO THE DEPTHS

They could have asked India, but she was too far away to offer support. Even if they weren't so far, there was no doubt they remained deeply embroiled in a war over Tariel's actions and absence. There was no possibility of meaningful help from there.

That left Arabia, though they were far enough away to be no more than a distant hope. Besides, Rostevan was unlikely to further support the campaign Avtandil had dedicated himself to. This much had already been established. With these thoughts, their talk began drifting in every direction. When it seems nothing is possible, one must consider every possibility.

Sometimes their discissions went towards the methods and means they might employ to rescue Nestan. Other times it was just a jumble of random and disconnected ideas and thoughts. But this is how people are. Their stress builds and boils, frustrated over a thing they cannot understand, or which cannot be accomplished. Then the pressure of their mind unseats ideas and facts from their roots, much like a river flooding its banks. When they finally understand or find a way to reach their goal, a flood of everything comes from their mouths.

It was in one such moment while Asmath was preparing meat over a fire when Tariel spoke up.

"There are many people in the world, but I never considered Nestan might be held captive by the Queen of Kadjeti. Until now, there was no connection in my mind between these caves and Nestan. But as you must know, the Devi are sworn enemies to the Kadjis. I may have an answer to our problems."

"You see, more than three Devi were here when we came. I can't say how many, but countless others occupied the halls and deeper parts of these caves. It took me days to slay them all."

"In all that time, I never considered what they were fighting to protect. Whatever they were defending did not matter to me. My two most faithful Knights lay dead at the entrance to these caves, and Asmath was shattered."

"All I sought was vengeance. In my rage, I bathed myself in the blood of those creatures. I only cared about embracing death or quenching the fires of my anger. But after days of bloodshed, I came to the doors of their treasury."

"However, I was unconcerned with jewels and gems. Wealth was of no value to me, so I never opened the vaults. Nor have I spoken of them to anyone. Not even Asmath. But maybe now is the time to see what's there."

"Do you remember those Kurdish brothers I met some days from here? And not only them but there are others too. Surely, we can raise an army. All we lack is the gold to pay for one. Let us look in this treasury. We may find enough gold to provide us with a solution.

The three of them rose from their seats then. They took

lights in their hands and went to the farthest depths of the caves. Asmath had never seen these places. Nor did she or Avtandil have any idea the caves went so deep or were so vast as what they now saw.

Yet Tariel knew. After nearly an hour of walking, they reached an enormous metal door. He had led them directly to their destination.

A beam of black ironwood thicker than the length of a man's arm barred entry. It was set into the stone walls at the edges of the door. There was no visible way to enter, but this did not deter the King of the Indians. Tariel drew his curved sword and hacked the wood to bits. As the last pieces fell away, the doors silently swung open.

Inside, there were many pieces of precious pottery. Some of it was impossibly complex in design. Other parts were painted in colors that appeared to glow and come to life. But this was just pottery. Despite Avtandil's disguise in Gulansharo, none of them were or wanted to be merchants.

And anyway, they didn't have time to barter goods. But there was another metal door at the end of the chamber. This one was a lighter color and similarly barred with black ironwood.

Once more, Tariel hacked the wood to pieces, and the door silently swung open. Behind this door was another vast chamber filled with different wooden furniture items. Like the room before, the things inside were impossibly beautiful and complex. Each was a work of art. But the knights had not come to appreciate the craftsmanship of Devi and who knows what else. They needed coin to fund a war. However, there was yet another door at the end of this chamber.

Once more, Tariel began hacking at the wood barring the way. This time Avtandil helped. Soon they made their way into a chamber full of wine and spirits. As before, there was yet another door barred with ironwood.

Working together, the knights hacked their way through this one too. Over the next few hours, they cut through many more doors. Each one was slightly different, and they all opened into rooms full of unique and wonderful items. Some were filled with armor of every style, carefully placed on shelves as though only waiting for warriors to wear it. Others were filled with swords, and another held nothing but bows and brilliantly colored arrows.

They found gold and silver beyond counting, with rubies more numerous than stars, and pearls the size of balls for play. But with each door they passed, their curiosity grew. Until they reached the last one.

This was the fortieth door, and it was made of pure jade. Ornate and lifelike carvings of what could only be the Devi battling some human foe covered it from top to bottom. A net of glistening adamant was strung across the whole thing, leaving no possibility of cutting through. Their only hope to gain entry was a large lock at the center. But there was no place for a key, and none of them could see any other way in.

CHAPTER 27 –

THE JADE VAULT

More curious than desperate, the three looked for a way to get inside. They thought there might be some trick to entering, for a lock seemed too simple an obstacle. Instead, their attention was focused on pushing and pulling at various parts of the carvings on the door. They hoped to find a hidden mechanism or pattern to show the way forward.

Avtandil was to one side, and Asmath at the other, while Tariel worked his way around the middle. But their search was fruitless. At least until Tariel's arm bumped the lock. When that happened, he shouted, drawing his blade, and whirling around. Yet there was no one there. No one, that is, except his arm.

The priceless golden armlet Nestan had given him writhed and twisted around his arm like a snake, seemingly brought to life by contact with the lock. In shock, he reached up and removed it. Asmath and Avtandil watched, equally surprised, as the armlet seemed to pull itself toward the lock. When Tariel brought the two together, the armlet welded itself into the mechanism.

With a deafening sound and a bright flash, the lock and chains disappeared as if they were never there. Tariel's armlet fell to the ground, and the door to the Jade Vault swung open. As it opened, the room was illuminated with a bright white and green glow. Unlike the other vaults, this one was smaller, yet every bit of the walls was made of the same jade stuff as the door. They were covered in carvings, which appeared to tell the story of great battles.

In the center of the room was a sealed green chest, longer and larger than a carriage. A golden placard was affixed to the middle, with writing in some foreign alphabet. But as the three approached it, the letters shifted into ones they could understand. It read, 'Herein rests the greatest of treasures. Armors impervious to damage and immune to sorcery of every sort, paired with swords that cut steel like cloth. Woe to those of the Kadj empire who make war upon the Devi again. Whosoever opens this chest for any other purpose than the death of the Kadjis is a slayer of kings.'

The three of them looked at each other in shock and surprise. They had no idea what sort of treasure they'd stumbled upon, but if it bore such a warning, surely it would aid their cause. Of course, no such swords or armor as the placard described existed. But perhaps they were possessed of other unique properties.

With eager hands and curious minds, they broke the seal to the chest. A rush of air came from within, and the lid lifted back of its own accord. From within, a green glow emanated. The chest's interior was made entirely of emerald and divided into three identical compartments. Each one held a breathtakingly beautiful suit of armor, with a matching shield and sword. Three suits of armor fit for three warrior kings.

The one on the left was black as night. In the middle, there was one with the same golden-orange color as the sun. And on the far right, the armor and weapons were pure white, like new snow under a full moon. Coats of shimmering mail, helmets, greaves, swords, and shields.

Each set and suit had a different design and style than the others. But all of them were of craftsmanship never seen before in this world. The emerald nests they rested in were like shrines to holy relics from a forgotten age.

Looking at each other, the three of them reached into the chest simultaneously, each taking out armor and weapons. Tariel was on the left and took out the black armor and sword. Avtandil reached in from the right, bringing out the glistening white armor and sword. Asmath, though no warrior herself, took out the golden-orange armaments. When the last piece was lifted from the chest, the emerald crumbled into dust.

While the three were shocked at what happened to the chest, they were more surprised by what they held. The armor and weapons were light as cloth yet firm and strong as the steel they appeared to be crafted from. Each looked at the other in surprise.

Asmath was the first to speak. Though no warrior, it was she who helped Tariel in and out of his armor each time he came and went from the caves. She knew the weight of such things as well as any knight and could not believe what she now held.

The heroes assured her that however beautiful these items were, they couldn't be real. They were clearly for decoration or ceremony, as no such things existed in the world save perhaps the veils Nestan wore. But her veils weren't armor, for they could be cut. After all, she'd sent cuttings to Tariel.

This meant they were not impervious to damage, as the now vanished placard had indicated. But the Knights still wanted to see how strong the stuff was. To test it, they put the armor on and took up their swords and shields. They laughed as they did so, for each felt he was wearing a suit made from cloth. Avtandil put down the white shield from his suit and picked up the old and battered shield he usually used. He shouted to Tariel, 'Come Icarus, and see how high you can fly!'

Laughing, Tariel took a fierce swing at the shield his friend held, hoping at least to knock him down. But something far different happened. Something none of them were prepared for. Avtandil did fall, but not just from the force of Tariel's swing. Rather, it was the fact of the black sword. It broke through the Arabian's shield and slashed deep into his side.

Asmath screamed, and Tariel ran to the side of his friend, desperate to undo his actions and rewind the hands of Fate. But the wound delivered was mortal. No man could survive such a blow.

CHAPTER 28 –

THE LAST HERO FALLS

U nfortunately, Fate is an unforgiving mistress. The evil she weaves tears and rips over the landscape of the living like a tornado. Her hand touches the brow of every man and woman, and like the shadow of old age, the ills she sows grow with time. Just as none in that room could stop the earth from turning and circling the sun, neither could they stay the hand of death.

But Avtandil lived, as evidenced by a cough and a laughing curse at his friend's expense. Asmath and Tariel could not believe he was alive. No man could survive such a blow, yet the Arabian was uninjured. Though he had crumpled beneath the force of the blow, and would be sore for weeks, he still breathed.

The sword had not damaged the armor, but it also hadn't cut through it. Clearly these armors and weapons were not decorations. They were crafted of finer materials and workmanship than the heroes had imagined. Whether they were impervious to damage and would cut through steel like cloth remained to be seen.

However, on the battlefield, all swords were the same. The only difference between one and the next was the person holding it. Novices defined themselves by their weapons and armor. But only master swordsmen could give definition to the tools with which they made war. And without the expertise of true heroes, these sets of magical armor may indeed have just been decorations.

But Avtandil was both hero and master swordsmen. So was Tariel, who had once fought the armies of Ramaz with only 300 Knights. God had given them all they needed and more than they could ever want. Weapons and armor fit for angels were in their hands. Now they had only to be about the work of He on High and rescue Nestan from the evil Kadjis.

The necessity of time left them no opportunity to leverage the treasuries of the Devi in pursuit of their goals. Nor would they be able to barter goods or seek out armies and armories. Their path was one of urgency, and whatever powers their new weapons and armor might possess, it would be their hands and determination which would determine their victory or defeat.

Tariel put on his new armor, and they left their old gear on the floor of the Jade Vault. Asmath carried the gold armor, for they would gift it to Phridon. As they left, they closed each of the vault doors. On their way out, they also took some bags of gold with them, along with rare pearls and gems. Avtandil spoke as they made their way up to the main caves.

"From this moment forward, our palms shall be wed to the hilts of these blades. Tonight, we will rest. In the morning, our road from here must not be delayed. We have far to go and much to do. Together, we will prevail!"

They all agreed and, after a meal, went to sleep.

Morning would come too soon, as it always did when great things were afoot. But that night, brother and sister slept, lovers of stars who none could equal. Brave heroes, all set to start on the road to Kadjeti, though none could yet have known whether it was they or their enemy who would be pierced by lances. As Fate is forever on the prowl.

In the morning, the two knights prepared themselves. They wore the armor and weapons of the Devi, Tariel in black, and Avtandil in white. Asmath carried the golden armor with her, which she had carefully wrapped.

The Knights took turns carrying Asmath behind them until they met a merchant and purchased one of his horses. Then she had her own mount, and the three rode long and fast. Eventually, they reached the lands just outside Mulghazanzar, where they saw herds of Phridon's horses grazing in the fields.

It was a pleasant sight to the three of them, who had ridden so long and far to reach this place. But then, at that moment, the idea to make a grand joke came upon Tariel. He turned to Avtandil and explained what he planned to do. The Arabian agreed, laughing at the boldness of his friend, and sharing the joke with Asmath.

CHAPTER 29 -

JESTER AND FOOL

"Listen, for with a good joke, even the proud are made to laugh. Avtandil and I will ride down the hill and seize the herd. We will chase off Phridon's herdsmen, and they will go to him for aid. No doubt he will come with haste, prepared to dye the fields red with the blood of those who have trespassed against him."

"Yet, before we come to arms, Avtandil and I will reveal ourselves. Phridon will see who it is before him, and his anger will turn to joy at the sight of us. We will all share a laugh, and his wild heart will calm. Then we will go to the city and celebrate as we share our news with him."

Asmath, though she did appreciate the joke, thought the two knights were behaving like boys. She said as much to them, but they just agreed with her and laughed. They left her on the hilltop and rode toward the herdsmen and their horses. As they drew near, the two men shouted, grabbing horses, and turning their weapons towards the herdsmen.

The herders, simple men, did not stay to fight. They ran, warning the two strange knights that Phridon was sure to come and spill their blood. But their words only seemed to provoke the two strangers, who released the horses and rode towards the shrieking herdsmen.

Though the knights stopped short of harming the herders, the men still feared for their lives. They fled towards the safety of Mulghazanzar, shouting and crying for the guard and their King. It was not long before Phridon heard of bandits outside the gates. He arrayed himself and twenty of his guard, riding out towards the intruders. A regiment of soldiers followed behind them, armed to the teeth. None had ever breached the city's walls, and none were going to – this day or any other.

The men of Mulghazanzar spread out across the field, with Phridon at their head. Two knights stood before him, wearing strange armor. One shining white and the other black as night. Helmets hid their faces, but it wouldn't matter. No two men could stand against the men beside him, knights or otherwise.

The two would-be bandits rode forward. They charged toward Phridon and his men but pulled up short before engaging them. Then Tariel turned, removing his helm and shouting.

"Look at you! What sort of host gives such a welcome? Are you so annoyed that you've brought an army to greet me on my return? Who meets guests to fight!"

Then Avtandil removed his helmet, and Phridon doubled his surprise at seeing them together. The three men dismounted, embracing, and laughing as they thanked God for the sight of one another. Many of the knights and soldiers from Mulghazanzar recognized the Arabian and the Indian. They came forward to greet the two.

Phridon asked what took them so long, for he'd expected to see them nearly a month earlier. He knew of their coming because of the message Avtandil had sent back from Gulansharo with his men. But now he saw the proof, as did all gathered on the field that day. It was as if two suns and a moon had reunited. Their beauty enhanced one another and was crowned by the sight of Asmath riding down from her hiding place.

The three knights and the maiden rode into Mulghazanzar at the head of what seemed a parade. People from every corner of the city gathered to celebrate the return of Tariel and Avtandil. Those who saw Asmath danced at the sight of her. A feast was ordered, and the four returned to Phridon's palace to prepare themselves and discuss events.

Once they were readied, a throne covered in golden cloth was brought forth for the King of the Indians, and the Arabian prince sat on a throne of emerald. Phridon seated Asmath beside him and then commented on the strange and wondrous white and black armors his friends wore.

They told the story of how it had been found in the caves of the Devi. Each took turns explaining how the armor was impervious to damage, and the swords could cut through anything. They gave Phridon the gold sword and shield when their tale was finished. Then Asmath gifted him the sunlit golden armor. Tariel and Avtandil were surprised to see she had woven yellow and white flowers into the seams. Yet, her adornments only served to further beautify and enhance the workmanship.

Tariel and Avtandil apologized for not having given him more. Still, they assured him there were many more incredible treasures in the caves they had come from. However, as they were currently about the business of war, other presents would have to wait. Now, all that mattered was the business of ruining their enemies. And gifts to support that cause were the best kind one could receive.

That evening they rested and refreshed themselves. For the first time in months, they enjoyed the comfort of baths and clean clothes. Phridon gave the men well-made pants and shirts, and his maidservants provided the finest dresses for Asmath to choose from. He further gifted them rare jewels and pearls in the morning, presented in their rooms on trays of gold.

When the knights and Asmath came down for breakfast, they began discussing the business of rescuing Nestan. Phridon did most of the talking, for he had not been idle in the months since learning of Avtandil's discovery. His men and scouts had gone abroad to seek information, which he now shared.

"It pains me to be a bad host, but I fear there is no other way than to speak directly. No doubt my speech will make it appear as though I have wearied of hospitality towards you, who are mad. But this is not the case. Rather, now is not the time to tarry and waste our time with pleasantries. I have learned much in your absence. But all is lost if the Kadjis return before we reach their castle."

CHAPTER 30 –

THE TEETH OF A LION

After a pause, Phridon called over his cartographer and several ship captains. He had them lay out maps and charts before speaking again.

"There is no point in bringing a large host of men to siege Kadjeti castle. It is a rock on all sides. There is no possibility of engaging the castle by force. Therefore, a large army is of no practical use. More, it is a hindrance, for our way and design will be plainly seen through the number of men we bring. Instead, we should only take three hundred men with us. They will be more than enough, particularly with us leading them."

"We will ready our swords for the assault but move upon the enemy with silence and stealth. Like runaways, we will be upon them before they know our numbers or intent. In this way, we will soon liberate her, who shames the aloe and cypress with her form. Our Tariel will be reunited with his nightingale and nest himself in the rose of her love."

Following his words, there was much discussion. Different ideas were put forth, some agreed upon and others discarded. Eventually, their plan of assault was decided. They would sail on fast ships, making their way directly toward the fortress of Kadjeti. They would travel by day and night to reach their destination in the shortest possible time.

Once they reached the far plains of Kadjeti, the men would stealthily disembark from their ships and carry on by foot, leading their horses. They would only travel by night, so none would know of their coming or going. Within ten days, they would reach Kadjeti castle. Knowing there was no possibility of openly engaging the fortress, they would take it by surprise. The three hundred knights would storm the gates as one, breaching the defenses and liberating Nestan.

All gathered agreed this was the best plan. So, the ship captains, cartographers, and generals returned to their quarters, leaving the three knights and Asmath alone. The four of them shared wine and stories among themselves until the hour grew late.

In the morning, they left, except Asmath, who remained behind. She was as much a warrior as any man there but not a student of the sword. There was nothing she could bring to this battle. Phridon, wearing his gold armor woven with flowers from Asmath's hands, gave her a gift and a kiss on the forehead in parting.

She stood at the highest balcony of his castles, watching as the ships loaded and left port. Three hundred knights, led by three heroes, would be spread across seven fast vessels. Together they would make their way across the sea, and God would give victory to those who had been unjustly distressed. As the last ship left port, she let a bright yellow silk cloth fall from her hands. It was lined in gold and carried her wishes for the safe return of Phridon, Tariel, Avtandil, Nestan, and all the knights they went with. At first, it fell, but then the wind lifted the edges of the fabric until it disappeared into the Heavens. It flew up to God with her prayers and those of the many women in the city. Together, they watched their men leave across the sea, uncertain whether they would ever see husbands, brothers, or sons again.

The ships, fast as they were, made good time on their way across the Indian sea and towards the lands of Kadjeti. The ship captains did not falter or delay their course. They knew the way and never steered in any direction other than their destination. In less than a fortnight, the ships arrived, wind and good fortune their guides. They came to rest on the far shores of the plains of Kadjeti on a moonless night.

The men disembarked, silent, save for the whispers of their breath and small talk. They made their way across the plains, moving in groups of thirty at a time to avoid suspicion or excessive noise. At night they stealthily crept forward, and by day they rested. They made better time than expected and were soon near the gates of Kadjeti.

True to what they had been told, it was indeed a fortress city. Rock surrounded it on all sides, with only a small way forward to reach three massive iron gates. Spikes rose from the walls like the teeth of a monster waiting to feast on the unsuspecting. And the sounds of men constantly on the march could be heard echoing from within the fortress.

All around Phridon's knights, bits of bones, broken armor, and swords littered the plains. Evidence of the failures of other armies to breach the walls of Kadjeti. Whether these heroes would succeed was far from certain, but the remains of those who had tried and failed were a sobering reminder of the task before them.

The number of men guarding the fortress could not be counted. There were too many. But one could easily estimate their number at well over ten thousand. Still, Tariel was undaunted. He had once led three hundred men against more than ten times this, and victory had been his.

The knights with them agreed. They were led by three heroes and would not falter. Yet there was a choice to be made. How would they assault the fortress? A direct attack was doomed to failure, for the walls were impregnable. But the moon shone brightly, illuminating everything. And in that light, there was a glimmer of possibility. For one hundred can overcome one thousand if they find the best way to do so.

CHAPTER 31 –

PLANNING THE IMPOSSIBLE

Lightning flashed far off in the distant northern mountains. It cast strange shadows across the fortress of Kadjeti. None of the heroes knew whether it was a good or bad omen, but the sight stilled every man among them until Phridon spoke.

"Brothers, I hope you will not take offense at my speech, but I do not think my words are out of place. Only three of us bear arms against this fortress. While we are supported by three hundred knights, there is no rear guard and no reinforcements. If we fail here, all is lost."

"The only possibility of taking this city by force would be with an army. But we lack the strength of numbers to directly assault any of these gates, let alone all three. I know our boasts and past accomplishments might wish to say otherwise."

"Still, there is no shame in being realistic about the options before us. Should the enemy shut the gates against us, our numbers could not overcome these fortifications in a thousand years. Yet, I have an idea."

"When I was a youth, my father had gymnasts instruct me in the secrets of gymnastics. I learned all their tricks, leaping and flipping through the air. After years of training, I could run along a rope so fast that the eyes could not follow me. All the other boys who saw me wished to do as I could, but there were none. I alone learned the tricks and talents of those performers."

"I say, whoever among you is best at throwing a rope, let him cast it onto the tower nearest to us. Though it may seem an impossible distance to you, it seems easier to me than crossing a road. The armor and shield you've given me are like cloth. They will not burden me in the least."

"I'll run across and jump into the fortress, laying waste to the men in the outer garrison. Then I'll throw one of the gates open, and we will begin to teach those within the lesson of their folly. What do you think of this?"

Tariel looked up at the nearby tower as Phridon spoke. The idea seemed sound. He had no reason to doubt the prowess of Phridon. Yet, Avtandil spoke against the idea.

"Hah! Phridon, you are a friend to whom none can complain. Your hope is placed in those massive lion-like arms of yours. It is true, no wounds will befall you, to be sure, and you will put any foe to rest who dares stand against you. But what of the noise you'll make while crossing?"

"The armor is light as cloth, it is true, but the jingle of mail and metal will give you away. Do you not hear, even now, how the men garrisoned within shout to and from one another? They will see you and cut the rope."

"Your armor will protect you from blades and arrows, but it cannot stop the earth. The ground will break you and your fall. Meanwhile, the men within will extinguish the light of your life. We will have no choice but to throw ourselves against them in a desperate and failed bid to save you."

"In the end, all will be lost. The brave deeds we hope to accomplish will go unfulfilled. She, who the sun bows to, will have no one else to save her. Only the vanity of our attempt will be remembered. My friend, let us consider another way to put your mighty arms to use."

"You all know it is not long since I have played the role of a merchant. What if you were to remain hidden, and I presented myself as a traveler? I could load some bit of our arms and armor, claiming to be selling fine wares. Then, when they were looking over the goods, I would strike. My treachery would be equal to that of the Kadjis, but the gates would fall."

"Certainly, those within would be hard-pressed to overcome any of our three hundred knights. But they would stand no chance against me, for I am a true hero. I need only put a blade in my hand to overcome the first of our enemies."

"Then their blood will flow like rivers, channeling the earth. I would break open the gate closest to me, and you all would join. Together we would storm the fortress and destroy our enemy. This is a better plan. What say you? Has either of you a more promising idea?"

Phridon agreed. His arms were large, and his poise and grace were without equal. But so, too, was the earth hard and unforgiving. If he fell, their plans would all be brought to ruin. Sending Avtandil in as a merchant seemed like a better idea. Or, at least, one closer to the earth.

But Tariel disagreed. Though he thought the idea was good, another matter concerned him. It was this that he shared with his friends.

CHAPTER 32 –

THE BUSINESS OF WAR

" Ah, my brothers. If any man in the world had the equal of you for his companions, surely his kingdom would reign forever. Your heroism is without compare, and the advice you give is as strong and well-measured as your own hearts. I know you wish to engage the enemy in true combat and not just vainly brandish swords."

"This character of yours causes men such as these knights to swear their allegiance to our cause. They see in you the will of heroes who will not falter or fail in what they seek to accomplish. This inspires them and gives wings to their bravery. No man can truly call himself a hero until his battles carry the peril of death. But, in this rush to engage our shared foe, you have forgotten me."

"She who maddens me and whose loss pains my every waking moment will be watching from above. My love will look down from the highest tower, like the sun. Her eyes will fall on you, doing the greater deed of heroism in your fierce fights, and she will see me sitting at the rear."

"To her, I will look like a cook, hiding behind the wagons of war while true and honorable men seize the day. This will be a slander upon me from which I could never recover. And I am better prepared now than at any other time in my life. For, at the insistence of Avtandil, I have spent this last year training in the fields."

"From dawn until dusk, I have worked myself into exhaustion. This fight was the sole purpose of my preparations and my entire purpose. But I understand. It is not only me who fights this day. We are all united to a single cause."

"No three heroes have ever joined together to a greater end than that which we seek to accomplish. So, I say, let us join our forces and bring the combined might of our arms against the enemy. Listen, and I will tell you how I believe we can best do this."

"First, we must divide the men equally. We will take one hundred knights each. Then we will separate ourselves from one another, approaching a separate gate with our men. However, this must be done at just the moment when the sun rises behind us. In this way, the enemy will not be able to understand who we are or truly measure our might."

"We will ride towards them peacefully. With luck, there may also be other traders or merchants on the road. Our numbers will mingle. No single captain can watch all three gates at once. So individually, they will see nothing in their watch too far from the ordinary. In this way, we will deceive them."

"Once our men are close, we will sound the trumpets. Our enemy will still be somewhat blinded by the eastern sun, but not enough to believe we are more than a minor threat. They will send out a small force of men to destroy what they believe to be insignificant foes."

"But they will not see the truth of our numbers. For this

reason, the wall captains will not order the gates closed. They must be ready to marshal more soldiers to engage our forces. This will mark the opportunity we seek."

"Only ten or twenty from each of our hundred knights should engage the enemy in the field. The rest will ride around them and make their way toward the three gates before they can be closed. The enemy on the field will be torn between engaging our knights and turning to chase us, which will cause their doom."

"When the men guarding Kadjeti fortress realize our true intent, it will be too late for them to close the gates. By then, one or all of us will have breached the walls. They will have no time or men left living to shut the gates at that point. In the worst case, should one of us be trapped within while the others are without, they can still break the gates with rams. What do you think of this?"

Phridon laughed when he heard Tariel's suggestion. At first, Avtandil was uncertain of why his friend laughed so much. Yet, the Lord of Mulghazanzar soon shared his mirth and, with it, a testament to his intelligence.

"Tariel, I see exactly what you seek to do yet fail to fully share with us. Now I am certain why she who loves you has eyes for no other. I know the horse I gave you cannot be stopped. Should it seek to ride through those gates, none can prevent it."

"Had I known we would be assaulting the fortress of Kadjeti, I should never have given it to you! The honor of the first assault would have been mine and mine alone! And besides, where do you believe we will find battering rams this morning? Hah! You are a clever man and a true rogue!"

Understanding lit Avtandil's face as he realized the truth of what Phridon said. For his part, Tariel turned just a bit red. And then they all laughed. Such was the strength with which their bonds of brotherhood were formed.

One brother could conceive the best way to do a thing he secretly wanted, and the others would laugh and then support him. After all, it was Tariel's loss that set the course toward this day in motion. He had carried the burden longer than any other. It was only fitting he should ride into Kadjeti first.

When the three finished their laugh, they began the business of dividing the knights into groups. Many of the men there carried horns with them. This would allow them to sound the charge as one when necessary, blowing again and again as they rode. Their enemy would further be confused by the noise. They would not know how many were coming or precisely from where because the three heroes would be striking from different directions.

Yet, the business of war is not all smiles and laughs. Though they shared a joke at Tariel's expense, each man knew he might not see the other again, as did the knights under their command. None were strangers to conflict.

They all knew the cost of war was measured in widows and cripples. Parades and holidays were just apologies to the survivors who silently carried the burdens of their nation. Today would be no different and no less costly to those who would not be coming home or seeing their loved ones again.

The three heroes embraced and clasped hands. Then each of them mounted, his knights falling in place behind. A final salute was their last gesture, followed by a raised fist, brought down to the chest before closing the visors of their helmets.

Each man then turned and rode away to prepare for the dawn and their final assault on Kadjeti. God willing, they would see each other on the other side of their individual battles.

CHAPTER 33 –

ALL THE MIGHT OF KADJETI

U nbeknownst to the heroes or their knights, there was
an alignment of the stars on that day. The Seven
Great Lights of Heaven were united with the will of God.
Stars of different colors illuminated the heroes and their
knights. And the earth seemed to glow in anticipation of
what was to come.

Tariel was poised to strike the center gate, black as
night in his armor and upon a steed of equal black.
Avtandil shone like a diamond, sitting on his white horse
as he readied his men to take the left gate. And Phridon,
brilliant in his golden armor, sat astride a tan warhorse as
he prepared to ride against the rightmost gate.

If their foes could have seen just one of them, they
would have been consumed by the sight. And what if it
had been possible for one person to have seen all three
heroes at once? That person would have become a sage or
saint at the sight, and the gates would have fallen without

contest. For none within would have been able to stand against the inevitable.

But the men of Kadjeti could not see. They did not know what was to come. The heroes rode towards the gates as agreed, and when the time came, the horns were sounded. Men spurred their horses forward, and as expected, Kadjeti fielded many soldiers. But they did not close the gates.

Like rain on a mountain, the approach of those three heroes and their three hundred knights started as a slow affair. The clouds spilled forth the bounty of their skies, and the trickle soon became a stream. That stream poured down the mountains, becoming a river and raging through the field and glens.

The knights now charging toward the gates of Kadjeti were no different than these flood waters. Yet, however fierce and tumultuous the rains may be before reaching the great waters of the oceans, calm ultimately prevailed. What raged and frothed now would soon subside. Whether in the seas of victory or defeat, none could predict.

This was the fate of wisdom, to be washed away by passion. For the words of philosophers fall silent beneath the footsteps of war. They cannot stop the inevitable any more than raised hands might stop the rain from falling. And from three different directions, the heroes approached the fortress of Kadjeti.

One man against each gate, leading one hundred men with him. They made their way forward without fear or concern. None could change what would be this day, and only the Heavens knew how it would end. At first, they came towards the gates slowly, their helmets covered with cloth to avoid raising any alarm.

Then, all of a sudden, they spurred their horses forward as one. The crack of whips striking horses cut through the air, accenting the blare of horns and shouts of men as they galloped toward their foe. From the fortress, countless soldiers spilled out, racing to engage the would-be attackers.

When the two forces met, the hand of God swept across the battlefield. The sweetness of the sun was darkened. And for the first time in recorded history, the wheel of the world turned against the Kadjis.

On that day, the wrath of He on High fell heavy upon those who held evil in higher esteem than good. All the might of Kadjeti could not contain the attackers. Life fled those sworn to defend the fortress gates, and the armies of the dead grew in number as the living were cut down.

CHAPTER 34 -

THE WEEPING WOMAN

The outer gates undoubtedly seemed impregnable to those within the fortress of Kadjeti. And the number of soldiers within was nearly uncountable. Then there were the sorcerers of the Kingdom. Every army that had ever assaulted the gates had been ruined through force of arms and dark magics. But this was not the case now.

Arrogance at their success in defeating every past assault had led the soldiers to believe they were unbeatable. Meanwhile, the sorcery they expected to fall from the Heavens did not come. Every Kadji competent in the dark arts was with the Queen, and they were months from returning. There would be no redemption from defeat for the soldiers or their captains. Instead, they would be visited by wrath unlike anything they had ever seen.

Although the knights who attacked the gates with Avtandil and Phridon were men whose valor and battlefield prowess were equal to the heroes of old, there was still the matter of Tariel. He was an untethered storm that nothing could match or measure. He carried the pain of years separated from his beloved in his heart as though it were a lance. Every one of his cries across all the nights he lamented the loss of Nestan gave an edge to his blade which could not be blunted.

As for the man himself, he was unstoppable. The cage of misery which held him captive for so long could no longer contain the weight of his wrath. He exploded onto the battlefield with a force unlike anything the men of Kadjeti had ever seen.

Those unfortunate enough to meet him in combat found their desire for battle fled faster than the courage they could no longer summon. Like the sun's brightness outshining the Seven Sisters of the Pleiades, none could withstand the intensity of his onslaught. His voice thundered down on those around him like the sound of God's flood as it cleansed the evil from the old world. Men who had not even been wounded fell to their knees in fear at the sound.

Faster than a scythe through wheat, his midnight black sword cut through men and horse alike. Chainmail and heavy plate folded and tore like parchment in the hands of a furious writer. All this was witnessed by those unlucky souls manning the walls. He and his force breached the center gates, and cries of terror went up from within.

At nearly the same time, Avtandil and the lion Phridon smashed through the gates on their sides of the battle. All who stood against them were battered and beaten aside. Some lucky few were tossed up and away, perhaps to have some chance of survival. But most were trampled into the earth by hundreds of iron-shod horses. So many fell beneath them that the legs of their horses were dyed red in the blood of the fallen.

But none stopped, and no quarter was given, even to those who begged. These were terrible men, and the worst thing a good man could do was to suffer the existence of evil. The heroes cut down every Kadji they crossed, leaving none living, at least not by choice. Before long, they made their way up the long tunnels to the castle, destroying everything and everyone in their way.

Phridon and Avtandil met in the center courtyard beneath the tallest tower. Their foe was wholly destroyed, and the fortress of Kadjeti had fallen. All was nearly silent around them. Save the moans of some few of their enemy who had not yet succumbed to their wounds, they heard no other sounds of battle. Men and horses were spattered with blood, and it flowed down the mountain tunnels in thick red streams. But the two heroes met with joy at seeing one another well and unwounded.

They looked around, seeking Tariel, yet he was nowhere to be found. Nor could they hear any sound or sign from him. Concerned, they rode to the far side of the tower, and there they saw the gates, smashed to bits as though the hand of God had rent them in two. Shattered bits and pieces of broken sword blades and armor were mixed with the mangled remains of those men unfortunate enough to have been charged with defending the gates. Clearly, this was the work of Tariel's hand.

It seemed like more corpses littered the ground than the stars lit the Heavens. Easily ten thousand men lay dead, more lifeless than the dust to which their forms would return. Those few castle guards who remained living were lying on the ground like sick men. Some held their insides together with bloodied hands, while others were left in pieces but still clung to life. None of them paid any heed to Avtandil or Phridon as they passed.

The two brothers went from one level of the tower to the next. On every new level, they found carnage equal to the floor before. Corpses were everywhere. The few men clinging to life held no more of it than a man with a handful of sand. They were not long for this world, but none Avtandil or Phridon asked could speak. The wrath of Tariel had left their minds as ruined as their bodies.

After what felt like hours of climbing from one floor to the next, the heroes reached the final floor. Blood and bits of what must have once been a man, or several men were sprayed across the room. But there was one door that was not broken.

They could hear a woman weeping from the other side of it. Yet there was not a whisper or sound of Tariel to be heard. Avtandil and Phridon turned towards one another, fearing the worst as they pushed the door inward, blades at the ready.

CHAPTER 35 –

A LIGHT SHINES

The heavy iron-shod door swung inward at an agonizingly slow pace. It made no sound as its opening revealed the chamber beyond. Avtandil and Phridon saw what neither of them had imagined, for there stood Nestan. Her body shook with sobs, and tears wet the floor where she stood.

Her face was buried in Tariel's neck, and her body was pressed against his as the two embraced. The moon was finally freed from the serpents and could meet the sun. His hair was thrown back from his face, and his eyes shone like stars as he held the woman who meant more to him than all the world.

It was like witnessing the union of Mushthar and Zual, Jupiter – the planet of Justice, and Saturn – the planet of woe. Or seeing the sun as its light surrounds a rose and the petals reflect their indescribably beautiful rainbow of velvet color. Avtandil and Phridon witnessed this as

Nestan and Tariel embraced, only turning away when the rose buds of the lovers' open lips became glued to one another.

To see them at that moment was cause for rejoicing. All the grief that until then had gripped the heroes loosened its hold. Their sorrows fell away and into the sea, disappearing into the depths like chains bound to an old and forgotten anchor.

It seemed the sun shared their joy too. For it shone through the windows of the chamber and across the room with blinding intensity. Nestan and Tariel were illuminated by it, lit from behind as though bathed in the glory of Heaven. This was when Tariel at last called to them.

"Brothers, do not be shy of us. My wrath is spent. And my anger has broken upon the corpses of those who dared to stand against us. Now is the time to rejoice, for our hands hold what all of us desired, yet none could have achieved alone. The glory of God shines eternal, for which we are forever thankful. Now come, and for we cannot linger here forever."

With those words, Avtandil and Phridon entered the chamber. They fiercely embraced Tariel, thankful to see him well, and then turned to Nestan. She called each of them, introducing herself and kissing them on the forehead as she thanked them for their service. She laughed and smiled, overcome with joy at seeing Tariel and happy to meet the men responsible for his salvation and hers.

Her laughing and joyous face was a light to the men, weary and tired from the arduous task of making war. But her soft words and smiles lifted their hearts. They enjoyed watching Tariel shine and smile. He was happier than either of them had ever seen. To their shared joy, the armor they had not failed. The three heroes had fought like lions, and their enemies had turned out to be goats.

Yet, joyous as their meeting was, talk soon shifted to the necessity of what they must do next. The surviving knights needed to be accounted for, and the fortress secured against any counterattack. To do this, they must descend the tower and begin preparations.

The four went down, wary of any of their enemies who might remain in hiding. The Kadjis were nothing if not treacherous, and the presence of assassins would not surprise the heroes. Yet they found no surprises. No more of their enemies faced them as they descended to the courtyard. And only a few still clung to life, but they left them to face Fate alone, as they deserved.

When the three reached the bottom, they found many of their men had gathered there. Soon, the number of those who survived was counted, though it was only one hundred and sixty. From three hundred, one hundred and forty had died in the assault.

Phridon grieved the loss of those who would not be returning home. Yet it only strengthened his resolve. He sent his remaining knights through every corner of Kadjeti in search of survivors. Every one of those they found who still lived had their lives extinguished until not a single Kadji remained breathing.

When this gruesome task was done, sixty men were assigned various tasks. Some would burn what remained of the castle defenders. Others would repair the fortifications and defenses. When these jobs were done, their entire force would guard the walls and gates until reinforcements arrived to relieve them. As they returned to the ships, the remaining hundred men would guard Tariel, Nestan, Phridon, and Avtandil. But before they left, there was still the matter of the treasuries.

Surely the Witch Queen of Kadjeti did not keep an empty castle, which meant there would be a vault somewhere within. But it was not just one vault the heroes found. Instead, it was a series of vaults that outnumbered and outshone the treasuries of the Devi. None who saw the wealth beneath the castle could imagine anyone had ever assembled so much gold and jewels in one place.

They gathered a second army of camels, mules, horses, and wagons to carry treasure. However, it was just the smallest part of the treasuries. They ended up with over three thousand pack animals and wagons. These were loaded with pearls, rubies, jacinths, emeralds, diamonds, and more gold and silver than a river could hold.

Once the caravan of treasure was loaded, they would leave. The heroes expected they would wind their way from the defeated fortress of Kadjeti and towards their waiting ships. But Tariel had another surprise in store. He insisted on meeting the Sea King first, saying he must discuss things with Melik Surkhavi.

But he did not tell anyone what those things were, and none dared ask. Everyone knew how Nestan had been treated in the Sea Kingdom. They did not want to stir the coals of Tariel's anger.

CHAPTER 36 –

THE INVITATION

Yet, their fears were unwarranted. Tariel rode on a cloud of joy and happiness that no one and nothing could diminish. Though he still wore black, gone was the morose and brooding knight once prone to violence. Now, a true hero stood in his place. Life and experience had polished the once brash Prince of India into a more mature and measured man. He sent a messenger to Gulansharo, and his words to the Sea King demonstrated this. They read as follows.

"Melik Surkhavi, from whose Kingdom the fair flowers of Gulansharo eternally bloom, I give you greeting. I, Tariel, destroyer of foes and vanquisher of armies, wish to meet you as my equal. Now I ride towards you, and with me, I bring the sun of my life, she whom the sight of pierces my heart with arrows."

"Behind me rests the vanquished fortress of Kadjeti. My knights guard the walls and man the gates, and the treasuries of the castle are mine. But I often think of how Fate casts her net over us all. My thoughts turn towards you and Lady Phatman. All the good I now enjoy happened through your hand and hers."

"Nestan Daredjan, the sun and light of my life was freed from captivity by Phatman. Then the Lady cared for her as a mother and sister. Meanwhile, the strength of your Kingdom kept them safe. My brother discovered news of her there, which he returned to me with."

"Without the strength of your rule, I cannot say what might have otherwise happened. But thanks to you, I am reunited with my love. But what can I give you to equal the joy your rule has brought back into my life? There is much I might offer, but I despise vain promises."

"Instead, when we meet, I will give you Kadjeti fortress and the entirety of their Kingdom. Accept it from my hands and post your men there to guard it, so the Kadjis never again darken these lands with their presence. I am sorry to be so abrupt, but we cannot delay our departure. There is little time for me to return to my own affairs, and I would see you before we leave the borders of your Kingdom."

"More, I would ask Usen, the husband of Phatman, to send her with you. No doubt she desires to see my beloved Nestan more than anything else. Hearing of her rescue will no doubt set the Lady's heart aflame. Let her come and be sure my beloved will also rejoice at the sight of her."

This message was set with a man on a fast horse. He rode unburdened by the train of treasure and without the need to provide a guard or escort for Nestan. Because of this, he made his way to the city of Gulansharo in less than four days. However, his horse was spent by the time he arrived. But he did not let anything delay his message.

When Melik Surkhavi received word of a strange messenger from distant lands, he immediately gave him an audience. On hearing the news this messenger carried, the King's heart jumped with surprise. The Kadji empire was his only and greatest fear. They forever chewed on the edges of his Kingdom, draining his coffers, and demanding ever-increasing payments to keep them at bay. Yet their soldiers did what they wanted to his merchants and men, and there was nothing he could do to stop them.

He found it hard to believe a foreigner had overcome the defenses of their castle and defeated the Witch Queen. But here stood a worn and clearly battle-weary knight as a messenger. The King needed no other invitation and thanked God, glorifying He who is just above all others.

He ordered men ready and prepared a retinue of his own. Outriders to announce his arrival and his personal guard to ensure they would have no concerns over banditry or the possibility of betrayal. Phatman came with him, and they brought many gifts, silks, and fine carpets on which to rest. Surely, they thought, Tariel and his men would not have such niceties with them. And it was the duty of one such as Melik Surkhavi to display his wealth and power when meeting strangers. However kind or well-intentioned they may be. A good ruler never knew when the hand of forbearance would need to become one of discipline. Because of this, he always maintained decorum, whether meeting strangers or countrymen.

They rode for ten days. Phridon's knight-turned-messenger also came, leading them to the place that Tariel had indicated. Their outriders came the day before, announcing the arrival of the King. This allowed the heroes time to prepare themselves, and when they saw the great King of the Seas in the distance, they rode out to meet him.

The sight of three lions with the star and light of the

Heavens caused Phatman to shout with joy. The King also rejoiced at the sight of them. Other than his son, he had never seen heroes such as these. And it had been long since his eyes rested on Nestan.

Now he understood the mystery of her sorrow when he first met her. It was Tariel who she longed for. He was the one to whom her heart belonged. This was why the flower and sun of the world remained darkened.

Yet they did not discuss these things at their meeting. Instead, the two kings dismounted and bowed, each offering their thanks and grace to the other. A host of troops formed a ring around them.

Some men were from the Sea King, and others were from Phridon's knights. But they all cheered Tariel. The men of Phridon were thankful for his leading them to victory. Those of Sea King gave thanks for his vanquishing of their foe in Kadjeti.

CHAPTER 37 –

THE SEA KING'S REACH

While the men cheered, Phatman lamented the fire burning within her breast at the sight of Nestan. She was unable to contain herself and soon approached the maiden. The two embraced, and Phatman blanketed the maiden's hands, feet, face, and neck with kisses before speaking.

"You are the sun of my life. In your absence, every waking moment has been less full than the one before. Yet the sight of you has lifted the darkness from my eyes like the sun chases away the night. No darkness can dim that on which your light attends. In the brightness of your presence, the full measure of good can be seen as eternal, and evil for the fleeting shadow it truly is. I beg of you, allow me to be your servant, and live out my days in joy by your side."

Nestan blushed at the words Phatman uttered. Her cheeks went red as the rose of her lips, and she put her finger over the plump lips of Phatman. Her whisper was hidden behind a smile, and the words that followed were sweet as nectar.

"You were the only one to carry my light through the darkness where I dwelt. Were it not for you, no hope of my salvation would ever have come. All the joy in my soul would have been emptied. I would have been forgotten, like the petals of roses falling before the freeze of winter. But God has seen fit to light the fires of my torn and faded heart once more. Where before I was empty, now I am equally full. The sun shines warmly upon my face, so you see the rose unfrozen, as it should be."

"In all the world, there has never been another like you to be my mother and sister. You will forever carry a part of my light with you. Every time I shine, it will remind me of you. I will hear your name in every smile I call mine and with each bit of joy that touches my heart. And for you being on the same earth as me, I will forever thank God."

"But your place is not as my servant. We are equal, though at different places in our lives. I can no more accept your servitude than you would accept mine. Though our flowers may occupy gardens across an ocean, they are no less free for it. Let us be sisters and visit one another from afar. This is a better measure for us than servitude."

The two women agreed to maintain their relationship as equals. They would write to each other from across the great ocean of India and visit from time to time. There were no shortages of ships crossing from one continent to the other, so it would not be a difficult matter. Yet, for now, they would enjoy the time given them by their meeting, however short or long it might be.

But their warm thoughts were interrupted. Melik Surkhavi had more to say. It seemed he was not content to let Tariel and Nestan leave.

The heroes looked around then, realizing what had been happening as they talked among themselves. When their attentions had been on their meeting, horses and soldiers had continued to arrive behind them. All of them were from the distant city of Gulansharo.

Concern and worry lining his face, Tariel turned and asked what was happening. But the Sea King just laughed. He spread his hands, as if asking forgiveness for something, and then answered.

"I am sorry, but it is not within my power to allow your departure from these lands. You must accept my apologies, for I cannot let you go."

CHAPTER 38 -

THE KEY TO FREEDOM

"Our custom in Gulansharo is to celebrate the meeting of new friends. The better the friend, the greater the celebration. I understand you must leave soon, so we have made some exceptions in your case."

"But now, Prince of India, you shall see the hospitality of the Sea Kingdom. I have commanded fine silks and tents for us to rest in. Meanwhile, a portion of the men from my garrison will pass by us from another road. They will relieve your men on the walls of Kadjeti. In this way, your men can join you, and they need not worry over your safety. For I would leave a guest like you without the guard due to his station."

"We will celebrate for one week, and then I will give you leave to depart. And what is seven days to us men? It is not so long. Did not He who rules on High fashion the entire earth and Heavens in such a time? Let us follow his example, and celebrate these days, in which time the creation of our friendship will be completed."

There was little Tariel or anyone else could say. One does not lightly refuse the Sea King. And besides, he was in the right. It was rude to leave so quickly. However, Tariel asked the favor of a ship on the seventh day so they could more quickly make their way home, to which he agreed. Until then, the heroes and Melik Surkhavi would celebrate.

Fine gifts were shared among them all over those seven days and nights. The fine silk carpets of the King were worn thin by their steps as they moved back and forth, giving presents to each other. Every treasure the King brought from Gulansharo was gifted, and gold coins were scattered in such abundance it seemed they would make a bridge from them. Yet some gifts from the hand of the King were more incredible than others.

For Tariel, he gave a priceless crown made entirely of the purest yellow jacinth. With the crown, he presented a throne of red gold, the likes of which none had seen before. Then, he turned towards Nestan and gave her a cloak. It was so beautiful she thought it might have been woven from the feathers of an angel.

When she moved, it shimmered and glistened, reflecting light from every angle. A rainbow of gems glistened and sparkled across it. Badakhshan rubies shone like red lights from it. She turned to Tariel, resplendent in her new cloak, and the two sat on the throne together. Their faces flashed like lightning, and those who looked at them found their hearts burned anew with fire. But the Sea King was not finished. His arms were wide, and he wanted to give more.

He clapped his hands, and two mighty steeds were brought forth. Each was saddled in finery, and with the horses, the King presented Avtandil and Phridon with several small precious gifts. Then he gave each jeweled coat, which shone and sparkled like the scales of some fantastic sea creature. They were unique and lovely as the heroes who now wore them.

These and many more fine things were exchanged. The Sea King continued giving gifts until it seemed he might next ask the oceans to pour forth their wealth of sunken and lost treasures. His generosity put many a kingdom to shame, and Tariel gave him thanks as only he could.

"Oh King, were I to spend a day in thanks for each coin between us, I might live to see the world born anew. Your generosity is without compare. I have never seen another so generous or kind in word and deed. Truly it is my honor and pleasure to have met you and enjoyed your hospitality. Thank God we did not pass too far from your Kingdom!"

"But let me give you what else I had planned, though it is not here with us. Beneath Kadjeti Castle, there are treasures that no man has laid eyes on before. It is like a sea of gold and gems churning beneath the fortress. Beyond us, you can see these three thousand pack animals and their wagons. But I tell you, a thousand times more could only carry off the tenth portion of that treasure."

"It is this which I give you. My rights as a conqueror to the lands and castle I have already given you. But also, I gift you all the treasures of Kadjeti. May you find years of satisfaction in emptying the treasuries that once supported your enemy. And should you need me, the Kingdom of India will forever be your friend and ally."

The Sea King smiled as he heard Tariel's words. The two of them embraced, and the King spoke.

"You who are the Lion of India, what will I do in your absence? These days with you in a field are brighter than any moment I can remember in my palace. I find life in your embrace, and the valor of your words and deeds quickens my heart. Many are those who sit now in my palace who will lament their Fate at not meeting you.

They will wish to have basked in the fire of your gaze!"

When the King finished speaking, Tariel turned to Lady Phatman. He took her hands, though she was shy to look directly at him, and pulled her close. To her surprise, his kisses fell on her cheeks, and he thanked her.

"To you, your children, and your husband Usen, I give all the treasure left upon these three thousand animals and the wagons they carry. But this is only material wealth. I am certain you can earn more than this a thousand times over. As honest thanks, I give you something more valuable. From this day, I have adopted you as my own sister. May you forever know welcome in my home and heart."

Lady Phatman knelt before Tariel, thanking him, and kissing his feet. Her words were for him and for Nestan, as his welcome was an invitation to see the lady whenever she wanted to.

"Many were the fires laid upon me at the sight of she who dims the sun with her brightness. Each day she was absent, I felt consumed anew. I feared the day when nothing would be left of me for those fires to consume. Yet now she is here and freed by you. My greatest joy is to see the happiness your embrace lays about her like a wreath."

"Until you spoke, my fear was to burn once more. But you have given me the key to my freedom. Now I need not suffer the fires of Nestan's absence. As your sister, I am blessed with nearness to the two of you. I will be a willing guest in your home and not suffer the woe of those removed from your sight."

These and many other similar words were exchanged between them all. In those seven days, they affirmed new friendships and made promises and gifts to one another until the seventh day.

CHAPTER 39 –

THE ROAD HOME

Then, out of necessity, they begged leave of the King. All of them had things they must do and places they must go. While they might wish to forever remain the guests of Melik Surkhavi and Lady Phatman, their duties would not afford them such leisure.

Nestan and Tariel jointly spoke to the Sea King. Their lips were like the rarest of red seashells, opening to reveal the crystal hue of their pearl-like teeth from within. As they spoke, it was as though the sun and moon stood beside each other.

"The absence of your laughter will leave us bereft of harp and song, but we cannot tarry longer. Though it may leave a pall upon our merrymaking, duty calls us all to different corners of the earth. We must beg you to release us, so we may go. Hope for us and what remains of our journeys, but let us make haste and find our ways home."

Though it pained him, the King gave them leave to

depart. True to his word, a fine ship had been provided for them and two escorts to sail with it. There was no shortage of provision or comfort on those vessels. In particular, the knights of Phridon were well pleased with their accommodations for the journey home.

Some of those who stood at the shore when the companions left wept at their departure. None had seen so many heroes in one place before. They knew they would not likely see another gathering like this in their lifetimes.

Of them all, none wept as much as Phatman. For her, nothing could equal the light Nestan brought into her life. She would miss the maiden dearly and count the days until they met again.

But the heroes must go, and so they did. Enough knights to man the two support vessels and provide an escort to the heroes came with them. The rest were sent back to the ships which had first landed. They took the main body of horses with them too, for sea travel is not particularly pleasant when one is accompanied by hundreds of horses.

That evening, three ships set sail. One large, and two smaller, easily moving through the waters between Gulansharo and Kadjeti. Behind them, the western sky lit with gold and fire. They sailed into the starlit eastern skyline. Most of Phridon's surviving knights accompanied them, save those who had gone ahead with the captains of the fast ships. Those men would go home first and share the good news of their victory with the town chiefs and the warrior clans.

Yet the three brothers were not concerned with the passage of time or any ship other than their own. They were too busy celebrating their success and reaffirming the love and devotion they shared for one another. Each swore their vows again, renewing their pledge of service to the cause of the others. Each night they sang and laughed together. Their voices danced over the waters and under the moon and stars as they sailed toward their destination.

Their celebration continued each day, and the weather over their heads never changed. Heaven smiled on their journey. The wind, which usually blew from east to west, blew steadily from the west, lending speed to their return home. Though their trip to the lands near Kadjeti took a fortnight, the way home took three days less.

When they heard the watchman cry out that land had been spotted, they let out a cheer. It was almost dark, so torches were lit. Bright beacons to keep away the gloom of night. They were reminders of home and lights to remember those who were no longer in the land of the living.

Soon the feet of those on board would walk on friendly lands. Their steps would no longer echo over the hollow wooden belly of a lifeless ship. And they would see those they loved and had missed. But no one on the ships knew how busy the men and women of the shore had been in their absence.

CHAPTER 40 –

WHAT IS NOT MINE

Messengers had been sent throughout the kingdom of Mulghazanzar to announce the victorious return of their King, Phridon. Moreover, he was accompanied by Avtandil, Tariel, and one hundred and sixty more heroes. In honor of the heroes and their victorious return, a celebration like no other had been prepared. However, the people aboard the ships did not know of this. They were expecting a grand welcome, but what met their arrival surprised everyone on board.

Before their ship was even docked, horns blared throughout the city, soon accompanied by harp and lyre, as men and women began singing. Fireworks lit the sky, and throngs of cheering people lined every space overlooking the harbor. Once the ship was moored, men from the castle came aboard. They lifted Nestan into the air, carrying her on a golden carriage.

The messengers who had earlier been sent to the lords of Mulghazanzar had not been idle. Nor had they forgotten Asmath, for she now stood at the head of a procession waiting to meet Nestan. People waved and cheered behind her, comparing the return of Tariel to that of a hero from the old world bringing the sun back with him.

His presence and that of the rescued maiden stirred a fire in the hearts of all who saw them. Those fortunate enough to look upon them that day would never be frozen again or left wanting of warmth. Such was the power of the King and Queen of India.

Though a tide of Knights waited to break free of the ship and into the waiting arms of their loved ones just steps away, the sight of Asmath stilled them. They did not move as she approached and lifted her eyes. She looked over those on the ship's deck, searching for one among them.

There, to her amazement, was Nestan. Asmath let out a cry and broke from the masses gathered on the docks. She ran to the ship, jumping into the embrace of Nestan. The two held one another as though they had been grown that way, like vine and tree, inseparably welded to one another.

Nestan held her long-lost sister, hugging and kissing her as the two shed joyous tears at the sight of one another. Her kisses lessened the weight of years, and the burden of loneliness etched over the face of Asmath. The service of her, who had given more than any other to Nestan, was finally finished.

A weight like the stone of Solomon's table broke, and Nestan spoke. Her words gifted Asmath a thing she had forgotten. This was the joy and freedom she had lost in her search for what could not be found. But Nestan was here now, and her voice filled the air between them.

"How might I speak to you of that woe my absence allowed to take root in your soul? It was never my intent to sow grief upon the fertile earth of your heart. I beg you, forgive me for this trespass. It was not of my own design!"

"Yet it seems God, in His infinite wisdom, has seen fit to grant us grace. The light of Heaven shines from above, and the earth's bounty is once more given unto us. But even if I live an eternity, I do not know how I might repay a heart so loyal and great as yours. Unless I were to give you your freedom."

"I cannot keep what is not mine. Though I am certain I will not live long enough to find a more loyal or devoted sister than you, it is beyond my means to chain you to me. Your service has been more than any other in all the world has known. As thanks for this, I give you all you might ask."

"More, even, for now, you have the freedom to do with it what you choose. You will no longer be my servant. But rather, my sister, more beloved and dearer to me than any born."

Asmath laughed at the words of Nestan. The tears of both maidens mingled, two rivers of different colors, twined together like the white and black Aragvi rivers. Yet their weeping broke of its own accord. Just as water on a leaf must fall when too much of it has accumulated.

Then, her hand wiping a tear away, Asmath gave an answer to Nestan.

"What words might I share with you to tell what my eyes have seen these many years? Understanding this sort of thing has not been something I previously sought, but Fate caused it to come unbidden to me. I could no more turn away from your need than the world might deny a new sunrise. Yet the death of so many years seems like life to me when I look at you again. Seeing your happiness fills and renews my soul."

"It seems I have been your advocate forever, and our years apart have not changed this. I am happy to see you with he who knows no equal and bows only before your heart. And you and I, who are friends and love one another, have now become suzerain and vassal."

"Ours is a shared labor, and it is from those like us which the best things are born. Thank you for my freedom, though, to be honest, some part of my heart will forever be yours. And a part of yours will forever be mine. Such is the way of things between sworn sisters."

When the two stepped back from one another, a cheer rose from the crowd. All the earlier service and devotion of men and warriors to their lords had been seen by all. Yet it was the threads of love between women which held the seams of it together.

The sacrifices of sisters like Asmath and Nestan were no different or better than those shared among the other women. It was their hands which rocked the cradles and tilled the fields. But more importantly, it was the strength and beauty of their hearts that sowed love and joy in all they touched. Without them, there would be no life.

But while some women welcomed their men home, others would never see theirs again. The pain of loss from some mingled with that of joy in others. This was a theme men and women forever shared. Some of them more than others. It was one such man who came forward now and spoke.

CHAPTER 41 -

HONOR THE DEAD

His name was Jemal, and he was a Chief among Phridon's lords. He kept the aviary where the hunting hawks were hatched and roosted. It was he who often spoke for many of the other men. As his brother had not returned home, he shared the sorrow of those around him. For this reason, it was he who addressed Tariel.

"We offer our blessings to you. Our people's knees have long willfully bowed in service, and God has given us cause to rejoice. For we, too, share your victory. Your face is returned whole to us without the blemish or stain of defeat. We are no longer consumed by the fires which burned us in your absence."

"It is said among the wise that he who gives a wound also possesses the power to heal it. Until now, we did not understand the meaning of this. Yet you, who wounded our hearts with your absence, have returned. Beneath your gaze, we are reminded of His divinity on High. We come before you with thanks for your return to our home."

With those words, each man and woman of those closest came forward. One at a time, they kissed the feet and hands of Nestan and then Tariel. This went on for more than an hour until their chief, who first spoke, came forward. He paid homage kneeling out of respect, but Tariel lifted him and spoke.

"Nestan and I thank you for your respect and homage. But it was for our cause your brothers joined the battle against Kadjeti. Tonight, there are those of your men who are not here. They paid the ultimate price, and their deaths weigh heavily upon me. But the sacrifices of those one hundred and forty heroes affords them an honor which is forever denied to the living."

"The eternally verdant fields of Heaven welcome them with joy and the light of He on High. They have become our vanguard and represent the best among us. Through their sacrifice, we will be reunited with the One, and the glory of their accomplishments will be increased a hundred and twenty times."

Tariel wept as he gave a eulogy for those one hundred and forty brave souls who had fallen in the assault on Kadjeti. They paid for Nestan's freedom with their lives, and he would celebrate with them again in the afterlife. Those who were related to the fallen wept loudest. Mothers sobbed, and tearful wives hugged children who would never know their fathers. Brothers and fathers held one another, missing a piece of their lives that no power on earth could ever restore.

Yet, though they wept, their tears were not bitter. They embraced their loss together. Those who had not lost someone helped to carry the burdens of those who had. But none forgot the victory that the sacrifices of the dead had won. For this reason, those who had lost kinsmen began a loud and deep chant. Soon it was joined by others until it became a cheer. For what better way to honor the dead than to celebrate how well they lived their lives.

In time, the cheering subsided into different groups of people. Each of them sang and chanted their own pieces of the lives lived by their lost warriors. The crowd was somewhat hushed when Phridon finally spoke.

"Our sages have likened Tariel to the sun, but through our deeds, his light is renewed. As thanks, he has given his eternal respect to us and to our departed. Let those of us here look upon this day with joy. Do not lament what was lost. Instead, celebrate and be merry, for victory is ours. And Tariel, do not hide your smile from us. This is the day of your return. Do not allow bitterness to sour your smile. Surely God will bestow a thousand more joys upon you and your beloved."

Avtandil agreed with Phridon and lent his voice to his cause. He turned and addressed not only Tariel but the whole of those gathered.

"The lost Lion of India has found his sun! You know how she vanished from the earth for so many long years. There was no sign or sight of her nor whisper, yet her song was heard from afar. Though she was held in a cage beyond men's reach, the bars were somehow broken. She was freed, and it is to you she came. Why, then, should any here find cause to weep? We enjoy the company of heroes who know no equal. Our hands together accomplished what one individual could never have done. Let us celebrate and turn the channels of sorrow from our eyes into tears of joy."

With those words, he beckoned to porters who came forward and lifted the throne on which Nestan and Tariel sat. They held it on their shoulders, carrying the youth and the maiden high above the gathered crowds. With careful steps, they made their way into the city of Mulghazanzar. The heroes followed, chanting, and singing with each step they took.

Their song was echoed by the crowds around them. Soon it was carried throughout the city, accented by the blare of trumpets and the rhythmic beating of kettle drums. People crowded the streets, throwing colorful scarves and bits of cloth as the procession marched through the city and toward the castle.

Merchants crowded out from their shops when they reached the main square and passed through the bazaar. People pushed forward in such numbers it became difficult for the procession to continue. Yet Phridon called out the people of his city, and they stepped back, allowing the heroes to continue. Whole families stood and watched as they passed, cheering the heroes of their city. They were all thankful to see Nestan and Tariel on their throne as it was carried towards the castle.

When they reached the palace, servants wearing golden belts and silk clothes of blue and white came out to greet them. They put down carpets of woven gold for the worthies to walk upon and threw gold coins into the air. So much gold was thrown up that it seemed stars fell from Heaven and into the joyous hands of crowds.

The sounds of celebrations and cheering people continued long after the procession of heroes entered the palace. Yet the events Phridon had planned were barely begun. Tonight, they would celebrate and toast to one another. But the following days would show the true meaning of hospitality in Mulghazanzar. This evening was barely the beginning of the celebrations to come.

Yet for Tariel, Nestan, Avtandil, and Asmath, the evening was shared with friends and fellow heroes. They traded stories and compliments with one another until the moon was nearly gone from the sky. Eventually, they made their way off to rest, knowing the next day would bring more celebrations.

CHAPTER 42 –

PHRIDON'S SECRET

Morning dawned with a cloudless and bright blue sky. This allowed the sun to illuminate every corner of the kingdom, and the light woke Nestan. She breathed in the fresh air and looked out her window, admiring the sea view.

On the other side of the room, Asmath slept, a slight smile tickling the edges of her lips. Her long dark hair spilled out over the edges of her pillow. Seeing her friend at peace made Nestan smile.

Hope was something she dared not dream of during her captivity with the Kadjis. Although Nestan only saw the Witch Queen Dulukhdar a few times, her presence meant the end of all freedoms for anyone she visited. Sometimes her thoughts still turned back to that evil place.

But she tried to scrub the memory of those dark and endless days from her mind. Instead, she focused on hope, which was an easy thing to do while looking out over the bright blue seas and white buildings of Mulghazanzar. But it still seemed to her as though she had woken from a bad dream. Because of this, she was constantly thinking of Tariel.

Though they had spoken, she knew there was much from their time apart he had not yet told her. She was also curious to know how her father fared or what had become of India, but neither he nor Asmath knew. They had wholly devoted themselves to the task of finding and rescuing her.

Now she was free, though it was still a new thing for her. Before her captivity, the idea of freedom had seemed such a small thing. Yet, in the light of all she had been through, its true meaning was revealed. Knowing the value of freedom meant she was truly free now.

Still, the taste seemed strange to her, who had been caged for so long. Looking up from her thoughts, she saw Asmath had woken. The two smiled at one another from across the room. They exchanged morning pleasantries and began preparing themselves for the day.

Phridon had sent them fine silks and clothes to wear, some of which were gifts from the Sea King. Nestan chose a dress of gold and red, while Asmath picked out one of blue and white. They helped one another to comb and braid their hair, refusing servants.

Instead, sharing their time alone as sisters are wont to do. When they were ready, the two came down. Ladies in waiting escorted them to their breakfast.

There, a feast had been set for them. Long tables stretched throughout the great hall. Every sort of pastry and delicacy imaginable had been spread upon them. Fresh and exotic fruits spilled from baskets.

The places were set with matchless finery. Amber and emerald plates had been placed for each guest, with gold and silver forks and knives accompanying them.

Flowers of every color lent brightness to the rooms, enhancing the beauty of the table settings. Their color and scent were matched only by the gardens of Gulansharo. And at the heads of the main table, three unique thrones waited for their kings and queens to arrive.

The center throne was for Nestan and Tariel. It was made of white ivory and deep reddish-orange coral. Gold and silver filigree were laced over the entire thing, while rubies and amber sparkled from every part.

To the left of it was a throne of rare yellow and black wood inlaid with onyx and tiger's eye. This was where Avtandil would sit. And to the far right was a throne of white and blue, covered in silver and platinum lace. These were the colors of Mulghazanzar, and it was here where Phridon and his guest would take their place.

Servants escorted them to their seats, helping Nestan to her throne in the center and seating Tariel beside her. Then Avtandil took his place to their left on his throne.

After this, and to her surprise, Asmath was called to sit on the blue throne. Phridon sat next to her. She blushed at the honor he bestowed upon her.

Then the minstrels began playing. Soon the sounds of sweet singing could be heard accompanying the harp and lyre of the musicians. People of the kingdom came in and took their seats, with thousands in attendance.

The food on the table was multiplied by an endless procession of servants bringing in fresh dishes. Meats and eggs, met with hot puddings and steaming cakes. It was a feast like no other, and the guests began filling their plates in anticipation.

Then, just as the last dishes were filled, Phridon stood. He raised a goblet of fine-cut crystal. With a smile, he announced a secret. This feast was to mark the commencement of a celebration in honor of Tariel and Nestan's wedding.

As lord of Mulghazanzar, he would be presiding over their wedding ceremony. The food was to ensure everyone had plenty of energy. For today marked the beginning of a nine-day celebration.

With that, he clapped his hands, and the feast began.

CHAPTER 43 –

EIGHT DAYS OF JOY

Nestan was so surprised she could not speak. Neither could Tariel. But in truth, all the heroes were caught unawares by Phridon's announcement. However, the lord of Mulghazanzar had spoken, and none could contest his will. Still, he explained his reasoning to his friends as the guests began to eat.

"You two have been separated for far too long, and it seems Fate has forever conspired to keep you from one another. But now you are in my kingdom, and I rule here. Your wedding will be presided over by me. Though you may have other weddings in other places, my hand will first unite you. There is nothing else I ask from either of you, and I am certain you will find no reason to deny me this."

This was how the beginning of Nestan and Tariel's first wedding was marked. None had planned it, but life is often less of what we planned and more of what we make from unfinished or unrealized plans. This day was no different. However, for the youth and the maiden, it was a dream they dared not hope to have.

Both knew the kingdom of India was in no state to host a wedding. And there was no other place where they might have been joined as husband and wife. Then there was the ceremony issue, as no one could preside over their wedding. Because of this, they hadn't even considered the possibility of marriage.

But Phridon was his own man, and Mulghazanzar was his city. While there was no one else they would have chosen to accept this honor from, neither of them could have asked for what their friend had given them. For this reason, his gift was the most incredible thing they could have received and something only Phridon could offer.

Once the breakfast feast concluded, the long tables were carried out of the hall. Then Phridon began giving gifts. At first, he presented fine and soft silks, which one could only obtain from the farthest reaches of the eastern seas. When Nestan ran her hand over them, a glimpse of pearl shone from the rose of her lips when she smiled.

From there, gifts and presents of every sort flowed from Phridon's hands to Nestan and Tariel like water from a mountain spring. Nine pearls were given, each the size of a goose egg. One for every day of their wedding celebrations. And then a gem which appeared to have been cut from the sun. This was placed directly into Nestan's hands, which shone and glowed like a miniature sun. The light from the gem was so bright an artist could have painted a picture at night using only the glow of that miraculous stone to guide his eyes.

On a different day of the celebration, Phridon presented Nestan, Tariel, Avtandil, and Asmath with necklaces so heavy they could scarcely hold them. These were made of gems cut into brilliantly glistening spheres.

Each part of the necklace was made from an entire jacinth. How anyone had found such an abundance of gemstones that size was a mystery. But it was only one of many secrets Phridon kept as he handed out more presents.

Phridon brought out a tray of rainbow-colored pearls for the lion of Arabia, which was so big it took two men to hold. They shone and glistened with colors ranging from the deepest black to the brightest white and every shade between. He gave them all to Avtandil before the man could protest. Then he followed with countless gifts of soft golden cloth and inestimably beautiful brocade.

Each morning there was a new feast, and every evening a different theme. Everyone in the kingdom and from the surrounding lands had come. Some guests visited more or less than others, but everyone visited at least twice. Gifts were also made to guests, lords, ladies, knights, and everyone else who came. The sound of birdsong was replaced by lute and harp, which never ceased.

At first, Nestan and Tariel had been shy of themselves. But by the third day, they had accepted their role as the center of this celebration. Now it was they who led the dances in the evening and made one toast after another as the feasting and festivities progressed. With sweeter words than any two lovers ever uttered, the youth and the maiden thanked Phridon. It was in his house where they were united as husband and wife. They lit the flame of eternal love in the halls of Mulghazanzar, where it would burn forever.

All was well and good for eight days. But on the ninth day, a problem revealed itself. Tariel sought the aid of Phridon, but it was a heavy thing that weighed on his mind.

CHAPTER 44 -

THE NINTH DAY

Tariel pulled Phridon to the side and spoke with him in hushed tones. His words were heartfelt and exposed a worry he had shared with no one else. In truth, other than Phridon, there wasn't another person he could have shared them with.

"Brother, your heart is more like my own than the heart of any other. Nothing I have or will ever possess will equal what you have given me. Not even my life would be sufficient to thank you. Nor would my soul."

"I tell you, when I lay on the steps of death, it was you who first gave me balm for my wounds. If not for your kindness, I might have ended my days like a ship forgotten at sea. I would have drifted until sinking or coming to rest into some foreign port."

"Sails torn and mast broken, I would have faded into ruin, moored to life by no more than the tragedy of my loss. There would be no praises sung of the deeds we have accomplished. None would remember the life I lived or know of my ending."

"Yet you refused to let me fall. In your heart, the fires of devotion never burned low. You kept true to the vows of brotherhood when almost everyone else I knew had died or been lost to me. Because of this, it pains me to ask more from you. But I need you to speak to Avtandil about a private matter."

"You know more of his sacrifices on my behalf than anyone else. But it is in his nature to sacrifice for those he loves. I want to ask him how I can repay his devotion to me and the cause of rescuing Nestan, but I know his answer. He will tell me there are no greater thanks than brotherhood."

"I agree with him in this, for it is what I would say if he were in my place. However, I also know there are things I can do to return the devotion he has shown me. But I do not want to unknowingly dishonor him in front of his kinsmen or the woman he loves."

"Yet, he may tell you what is in his heart. And if he does not, you still might find the answer between his words and vain denials. Then we can discover how I may serve his and his beloved's cause. For the measure by which each of you endeavored to quench the fires in my heart has been equal. Yet I know how to thank you, as you will see in time."

"However, Avtandil's heart is another matter. I know he desires something, but I cannot discover it. I am sure you have seen it too. Sometimes his eyes reveal a hidden thing when he looks across the room or stares off into places other than where he sits."

"I would serve this hidden cause of his. But, as he does not speak of it, how can I? You must learn the secret of it. Ask what will repay the grief he has endured for my sake. Tell him we know God will forever shine His grace upon the house of Arabia for the sacrifices he has made. But there must also be something I can do. If there is not, then I will forsake my own Kingdom. I will never see my house again nor step foot in India for the rest of my days."

"If he requests nothing of me and will not tell you how I can help him, then tell him my choice. And in this case, I will go with him to Arabia. I would see him united with his wife, as I am with mine. But he must guide me, for I do not remember the way."

"If he refuses, tell him I will be no husband to my wife until he and Tinatin are united in their marriage. I will see his Kingdom and happiness fulfilled, or not look upon my own again. He may try refusing what you ask but let him know I will not be denied. The choice of words or swords is his. We bring the sweet to reason with words and with swords, those who wish to fight."

CHAPTER 45 –

THE WILL OF A KING

With the words and wishes of Tariel fresh in his ears, the lord of Mulghazanzar went to find Avtandil. He found the young knight sitting with minstrels, playing the harp, and singing with them. His sweet voice carried the highest notes, and Phridon waited for the song to finish before asking to speak in private.

When Avtandil heard what Phridon wanted, he laughed at the seriousness with which his friend had approached him. The joy and mirth of the youth's smile brightened the room. There was no bitterness in his words as he answered. Instead, they were full of light.

"What reason do I have to ask for help from anyone? Surely, were I in need, you and Tariel are the first people I would ask for aid. But I am not troubled, nor do I bear any wound. The Kadjis have not taken my sun from me, and she does not suffer for want of joy. Rather, it is quite the opposite."

"My sun sits upon a throne for which there is no equal in all of Arabia. Her rule is ordained by the will of God. Our people respect and honor her, and none are more powerful. Wizards have not stolen the light of life from her eyes. There has been no tragedy to threaten the kingdom, for it is well kept by Shermadin and the armies he commands in my absence."

"In all these years, I have not suffered my own tragedies. To be sure, the pain of separation has worn on me. But all my steps have been taken with the blessing of Tinatin. Why should I ask for any help with her? Truly my friend, do not expect me to answer a thing which is not needed with flattery."

"One day, my life will come to an end. The light of Heaven will shine down upon me. If it is the will of God, then angels will visit my heart. I will rest before He on High, and all the fires and tragedies of my life will mean nothing. Whatever I am or have been will be illuminated by a thousand shining suns."

"All my wants and desires will cease to exist. For no shadow of mortality can withstand the light of His presence. Until this day, why should I waste my energies chasing after those things already in my hands?"

"Though I love you and Tariel the same, you must know the vanity of what you ask. I am satisfied with what I hold and call my own. Nothing more is needed for my sake or that of my beloved."

"Tinatin and I share a happiness I cannot describe, but we cannot keep such things to ourselves. The warmth we take from our union grows cold in the shadow of friends in need. All our sweetness turns bitter with the absence of joy in those we love. However great Tariel's compassion for me is, he must understand this."

"I hear his wish in your words and know he would see me wed to my beloved. This is a thing I also look forward to, but it will come with time. One does not rush the blossoming of a rose. Nor can they speed the making of honey from a bee. The tongue holds no sway in these matters, and the sword does not avail. Only through the will of Providence is the divine possible."

"But there is more we have yet to accomplish. The throne of India still sits empty. Let me be no more than earth until Tariel is restored to his rightful place as King with Nestan for his Queen. Let their foes be so utterly ruined that none dare challenge his rulership again. This is what I wish."

"Only when these things have come to pass can I allow myself the liberty to partake of my desires. On that day, I will return to my beloved in Arabia. The light of her sun will once more warm my heart. And if she wills it, the burning of my own fires will be quenched."

"There is nothing else I want. You know this of me. I despise flattery, for it dulls the blade of action. So, let us not make idle wishes and promises of futures we have yet to realize. Instead, we should take up the fires of those causes for which we burn and see them realized!"

"Take these words. Return with them to Tariel, for he knows the truth of what I say. I want many things, but time will see them all in my hands. Until then, I desire nothing more than to serve the cause of my sworn brother and his wife."

Phridon listened intently as Avtandil spoke. He noted every word, asking questions in some parts while agreeing with others. In the end, he returned to Tariel and shared what he had learned. The Indian laughed with love and admiration as he answered.

"It seems our friend has no time for himself, so busy is he with forever saving those he loves. Yet, reclaiming the throne of India can be done without the help of wizardry and sorcerers. Strength of arms and attention to duty will suffice, which we are not lacking."

"He has returned the light and love of my life to me. Nestan may have been forever lost without his aid and with her any hope of my own salvation. Though he speaks of his deeds as a small matter, we all know differently. If he will not reward himself, then the task falls to me. I will show him the valor of a brother and use my position to his favor."

"The time for 'if' is passed, and now is the hour of men. It falls to us to act, and so we shall. Return to Avtandil and tell him this."

CHAPTER 46 –

RETURNING TO ROSTEVAN

"'I will not return to India until I meet the King of the Arabians. Many of his men lost life and limb by my hand. I do not take pride in my transgression against his rule as King. When I see him, I will do no more than beg forgiveness for what I have done.'"

"'If the King of the Arabs will not listen to my words, then I will beg his daughter Tinatin. Is she not equally King? Of the two, surely one will find it in their heart to forgive me. If not, then I shall beg and persuade until they have agreed.'"

"'Do not think these actions are done out of adoration. They are not. Rather, this is an apology your two Kings deserve from me. My actions robbed them of their servants and the light of your presence. I will accept no challenge to this decision, for it is my desire and will. Tomorrow morning, we leave Mulghazanzar for Arabia.'"

Phridon listened to Tariel. Then he went back and told the youth what the King of the Indians had decreed.

Avtandil protested, but Phridon told him the decision had been made and tried to calm his friend.

"You know well the heart of Tariel. He will not remain here. But there is more. The three of us are friends, yet you forget that he and I are kings. What he says is not from a friend's mouth but rather the word of a King. Remember how respect is due to Kings and devotion to their rulership expected of knights. This is the way of things."

Yet Avtandil did not want this help. He needed no hand to assist him in Arabia. The fires of worry began burning his heart. He worried about Rostevan's anger. What would he do if his foster father and Tariel came to blows or were set against one another? How could he be true to Tinatin if her heart turned sour towards the King of the Indians?

Concern etched across his face, Avtandil went to beg Tariel to change his mind. He got down on one knee and pleaded with his friend. His eyes did not come up from the ground, and he kissed the feet of the Indian King as he spoke.

"I beg you, stay your course and steer clear of Arabia. You do not know what sins I have committed against Rostevan this year. Do not force me to break my oaths and betray my loyalty."

"I cannot know how he will receive you. Perhaps with love, but what if his hand is raised against you? You would put me between a rock and the earth, for I must choose between my foster father and you. Do not force me to cause Rostevan more pain. He is already pale because of me and the hurt I have caused him. How can you ask the servant of Arabia to use a sword against his master?"

"Whatever you desire will not be given by God's justice. There must be another way. This deed may cause a rift between Tinatin and me. She will see me as arrogant, and her heart will rise against me in wrath. I will be denied the sight of her and become a stranger to my own house. Everything I love will be lost. None but me can beg forgiveness for what I have done. Please, do not take this from me."

It seemed to Tariel there was no more honest or humble man in the world than the Arabian kneeling before him. He laughed with joy at knowing what a genuine heart his friend carried. His smile shone like a radiant sun as he lifted Avtandil up and set him on his feet, gently admonishing him.

"My friend and brother, your heart has done nothing but good for me. Through your deeds, my every joy has been returned. But without you, how can I truly rejoice? Let us meet your Tinatin, and then we will celebrate together!"

"You know how I despise fear in a man and dislike overmuch respect for ceremony and decorum. Majesty and gloominess are chains I wore for too long. Now I find their touch to be hateful. Do not burden yourself with worry. If someone would be my friend, let him wend his way towards me. Let us be apart if not, for separation is better for us both."

"I know how the heart of your beloved bends towards you. Do not think my years of isolation have made me forget what it means to know love or recognize it in another. Her hand is apparent in your every action, plain for us all to see. She will not be displeased at the sight of me. This much I am certain of."

"Of Rostevan, I cannot truly say how he will receive me. But we are both kings and can speak to one another as equals. I will address him respectfully, for he should give his daughter to you of his free will. There must be no compulsion from me or any other, as there was with Pharsidan when I desired to wed Nestan."

191

"But every father desires a son in the man his daughter marries. Just as every mother hopes for a daughter in the wife her son takes. In the end, they both hope to see a union that will bring joy and happiness to their children. Knowing this, how can you continue to endure the pain of separation?"

"Seek the hand you desire. Beautify yourselves with the presence of one another. Do not fade apart, or all the stars of your skies will forever dim. As for me, I want no more than to see the sight of Rostevan and Tinatin before my return to India. Would you deny me this?"

Looking into Tariel's eyes, Avtandil saw the truth and sincerity of his words. He understood his friend would not be dissuaded or turned away from seeing Arabia or meeting Rostevan and Tinatin. At last, he gave his assent and accepted the will of Tariel.

It was not the first time he had been unable to change the mind of a King. If Tinatin accepted him as her husband one day, he expected it would also not be the last. But that was a bridge he had yet to cross.

He only requested to wait a day or two more before leaving. This was so they might be better prepared for the journey. Only he knew how long the road was, and no other but him could show the way.

CHAPTER 47 –

THE SECRET GIFT

Over the following days, Phridon readied his men for the long journey to Arabia. He selected the finest knights he had as an escort, the same men who survived the assault on the fortress of Kadjeti. His men arranged wagons and pack mules to carry supplies and a carriage for Nestan and Asmath.

As he oversaw the preparations, he thought of what the sage Dionysius wrote. The words gave him hope for all their futures, and he quietly recited them to himself.

"We must forever remind ourselves that God creates no evil. His hands diminish the length of all bad things, renewing what is good. He is the eternal sun and perfection of self, forever becoming more perfect and never diminishing."

These thoughts held his mind as he prepared for their journey. Porters and knights came, and wise men consulted him to ensure the kingdom would be well cared for in his absence. When everything was ready, he announced the day of their departure to the people. The citizens lamented the time their King would be gone, but he promised to return soon with news and gifts from the far lands of Arabia.

The morning of their departure dawned bright, without a cloud in the sky. Three lions set forth, flanked by one hundred and sixty knights. Each of them was a hero and was sworn to protect the men they called lords and kings. With them came the ladies, riding in a gilded carriage drawn by brilliant white horses.

Nestan Daredjan was first, she who was the joy and amazement of all who looked at her. Her hair was darker than a raven's tail, with curls kissing the edges of her crystal cheeks. The ruby of her lips caused many an onlooker to gasp, and her smile revealed rows of brilliant pearls to those fortunate enough to see her. She was the bride of Tariel and the princess of India.

With her came the wise and devoted Asmath. She had forever sworn herself in service to Nestan and knew tragedy as few in the world ever would. By choice, she came, only recently released from her vow of servitude. Yet she also wanted to be close to Phridon. The two ladies shared the carriage, and the men rode before them to be sure the way was safe.

The people of every land they rode through welcomed them with gifts and celebrations. The blood of those who laid eyes on the knights flowed more strongly. And those lucky enough to catch a glimpse of Nestan found their hearts fuller. The heroes and maiden were a joy to all who saw them, and none were shy of their affections.

In truth, many a poet was made in the wake of their passing. It was as though the Nestan were the sun. She was set in a sky of moon and stars, surrounded by men of equal beauty and character.

For nearly four months, they journeyed. Each night

they celebrated their companionship and love of one another. This went on from the end of autumn through the entirety of winter. Until the first flowers of spring marked their arrival into familiar lands. These were the tracks near where Avtandil had once come, though it would still be months until the roses bloomed outside the caves.

Tariel also recognized where they were, and they alerted the knights. Within a fortnight, they would arrive at the caves of the Devi. Once there, the men would continue their journey to Arabia. Yet, Phridon was confused. He asked why they were traveling to a place other than Arabia.

This was when Avtandil spoke up, laughing as he shared his secret.

"Ah, my friend. Did you think it was only you to whom Tariel had a measure of thanks to give? In this place, you will find the reward he promised you before your conversation with me. A conversation, I might add, which resulted in this journey to Arabia. So be patient, and soon all will be revealed, much to your joy and amazement, I am certain."

Though unsure of where they were, Phridon trusted his friends. He wanted no reward, but judging from their surroundings, he thought whatever it was would be manageable. However, he would soon learn just how wrong he was.

CHAPTER 48 –

WHAT LIES BENEATH

They reached the caves of the Devi early one morning, and Tariel finally spoke up. He gathered the knights and porters into the clearing outside the mouth of the cave. There, he announced where they had come and what their purpose was.

"Friends, it now falls to Asmath and me to be your hosts. Beyond these doors lie the caves of the Devi. These next few days are my last in this place, and I will not miss it. The madness of separation afflicted me when I was last here, and I would not be reminded of that pain again."

"Yet we have stores of smoked meat inside, thanks to the work of Asmath. More, there are treasuries within which you cannot imagine. As I say these words, I know many of you may think I boast, for you believe yourselves able to imagine treasures. But you are mistaken. Of this, I assure you. As the last prince of India, I was gifted the one hundred keys to our treasuries, which you also cannot imagine. Yet, what lies within these caves is not even the tenth part of all the treasure in India."

"First, we welcome you into these halls, which were hollowed out by the magic of Devi. They are vast, so be careful you do not become lost within. Despite the many years I spent here, I have yet to explore them all. Eat and relax. Bathe yourselves in the hot springs, and rest. When all have sated themselves, I will show you the treasure of which I speak."

At his request, the men came in and refreshed themselves. Nestan, curious to see where Tariel had spent so much time, also inspected the caves. But she also saw the pain on his face at returning there and took his hand in hers. Gently, she pulled him aside and reminded him to be thankful for all God gives, good and bad.

"My love, we are only human. Though a divine spark resides within each of us, it is beyond our ability to understand the will of God. Had these caves not been home to you, perhaps Avtandil would never have found you or me. In this case, our story may have ended differently, and perhaps in tragedy for us both."

"Rejoice in the light and life Heaven has seen fit to provide us. And remember, all that is good comes from God. Let us not repay Him or these men who are so faithful to you with bitterness and regret. Rejoice, for we are reunited. Put your sorrows aside and let your heart smile as it did the first time you saw me."

Remembering her as she was and seeing her now with him as his wife, Tariel smiled. The pain in his heart was still. Once more, he was reminded of Nestan's wisdom. In all the world, nothing was more important to him than her. Nor, he imagined, would there ever be.

By early afternoon the knights and porters had refreshed themselves and eaten. Their meal was filled with excited talk of the caves and the prospect of seeing

Arabia. Everyone had stories to tell and tales of adventures they shared. Many a glass was raised in honor of God, who had turned the woe of their heroes into joy.

But the afternoon's highlight came when Tariel told them how he overcame the Devis who hollowed out the caves. He ended his tale by pointing down a long, dimly lit hall before speaking.

"Who among you is ready to see what lies beneath?"

CHAPTER 49 –

THE WRITINGS OF THE DEVI

A cheer went up from the knights at the prospect of seeing the wonders of the Devi. Nestan was also interested, for Tariel had told her how the armlet she gave him was the key to unlocking the armor used to defeat the Kadjis. This fascinated her, and she was curious to see what else lay within the forty rooms.

Tariel led the way, with Avtandil and Phridon following. Nestan and Asmath came behind and were followed by the remainder of the knights and porters. There was some talk among the men about whether they could fit so many people into the caves. But all such conversation ceased when they entered the first room of the treasuries.

Another hundred men could have come in riding horses, and there would have been space for more. No one could believe how big the first vault was. Nor could they count the number of items in it. One pair of eyes could not see everything in the room with one look.

They explored the treasure halls and vaults for nearly three days. Joyous shouts went up from the men as they saw each new room. Before long, they were making wagers about how big the biggest pearls would be or which golden chalice might hold the most wine. Meanwhile, Tariel enriched every man there with priceless gifts. But however much he gave, the treasure seemed untouched and uncountable.

When they finally reached the last room, Tariel handed Nestan his golden armlet. She used it to open the door, giving a little shout as it jumped from her hands and into the lock. Those gathered looked on in amazement as they saw the magic of the armlet at work.

But when the doors opened, those who had not seen it before gasped in awe. No one there had ever imagined such a place could be possible. Some few of them even wept at the beauty of it.

All the while, Tariel had been carefully watching Phridon. He knew his friend was not greedy and had no concern with collecting or hoarding wealth. Yet it was not wealth he wanted to give the man. Instead, his gift was culture and history, and he was not disappointed by his friend's reaction.

Phridon ran his hands down the carvings on the walls. He marveled at their intricacy and perfection, wondering aloud what the writings could mean. His excitement was so great he seemed to have forgotten everyone else in the room until Tariel spoke to him.

"My friend and brother, there are no gifts on this earth I might come to possess that could repay the debts I owe you. Long have I thought about what I could give you as thanks, but until this moment, I was not certain how my gift would be received. Yet now I see how much you are interested in these caves, and I am certain my decision is a thing you will not be shy of."

"It is said by many that a man who does good deeds will not lose in the end. And I will see no deeds in this lifetime to compare with those you have done on my behalf. Therefore, as thanks for all you have done to help me and Nestan, I give you these caves. All the treasure and history within them is yours."

"Take all you have seen and whatever else you may find in this place's deep tunnels and corners. How you will move it all, I cannot imagine, but I am certain you will find a way. You may find a willing hand from the Sea King, Melik Surkhavi. We know well his fondness for treasures and wealth."

"But whatever you do, and by whichever means you accomplish it, these caves I once knew as both home and prison are yours. May you find every kind of good thing to be done with the wealth herein and perhaps learn the secrets hidden in these writings. I wish only the best to you, my friend and brother."

Phridon looked at Tariel with a mixture of surprise and joy written across his face. The treasures here were so vast they couldn't be kept, even if he converted his entire kingdom to a treasury. But far more important to him were the writings and carvings of the Devi. He was sure there was knowledge hidden in them. All he needed were time and scholars to unlock it. His thanks to Tariel were boundless, and his voice shook with joy as he spoke.

"There is no greater ruler in the world than the King of the Indians. You who dispense wealth and kindness with the same hand cannot be adequately thanked or praised. In truth, none can stand against you, be they friend or foe."

"Your enemies bend and break like straw beneath the strength of your hands. And friends are made servants to your heart through the generosity and kindness of your spirit. May your kingdom endure for an eternity, as I will forever find joy and happiness at the sight of your smiling face."

This was how the caves of the Devi came to belong to Phridon. It would take many years of men and pack animals working day and night to transport all the treasure from the forty vaults. However, the writings of the Devi were far more interesting to him, but that is another tale. Before it could be told, he first needed to help Tariel return Avtandil to Arabia.

CHAPTER 50 –

TWO KINGS AND A KNIGHT

Phridon left some men to guard the Devi caves. Others were sent back to Mulghazanzar to arrange caravans to transport the treasures. The only task left was to make their way to Arabia. Tariel would accept no denial of his wish to meet Rostevan, so the men and knights not assigned to guard the treasure began their journey.

For Avtandil, he felt his return home was measured in suffering equal to that he'd endured when first searching for Tariel. All his longing and love for Tinatin returned with renewed intensity, eating away at his heart and soul. He became like the moon, growing less bright each day until it seemed he might disappear.

He also secretly carried a burden of shame and guilt over abandoning his duty to Rostevan and the people of Arabia. Though his friend Shermadin could protect the kingdom, it was not his responsibility. Avtandil was the sole person who carried that weight, and abandoning his duties hung a weight around the young knight's neck. A weight that grew heavier with each step he took closer to home.

Self-doubt gnawed at his courage and slowly eroded his resolve as the months passed. By the time they reached the towering walls of the Arabian frontier, Avtandil was ashamed to even show his face. Instead, he covered his head so no one would recognize him. Instead of the hero announcing his return, it was Tariel and Phridon who introduced themselves as rulers interested in meeting Rostevan.

The guards opened the gates and let the two Kings in with their retinue. But once inside, Avtandil's shame only deepened. Everyone he saw wore the blue and green of mourning.

The people of Arabia had measured and counted Avtandil's absence and feared his death. Each citizen shared the pain of losing their beloved hero. Yet there was no closure for them. Instead, they remained trapped in a purgatory of hope for the impossibility of his return.

His guilt only increased as they traveled toward the center of the kingdom. The people of every town, city, or village they passed through wore the same blue and green colors. It seemed as if every corner of Arabia missed him. There was nowhere he might go to escape the shame gnawing at his resolve.

After two weeks, they came to a hilltop from which the distant palace of Arabia could be seen. Tariel estimated it would take half a day to reach it, so he called messengers to his side. These men would carry his words to the King of the Arabians. They listened intently as he spoke.

When he finished, they rode off towards the palace. On their arrival, they were brought before the King. He ordered them to speak, and they dutifully related Tariel's message to Rostevan.

"Great ruler of the Arabians, I am King of the Indians,

come before you full of desire and hope. I seek an audience in your royal court, where I will present you with the rosebud, unfaded and unplucked. Though you will not know me by name, I am certain you know me by deed."

"It was I who once caused your anger on the fields. We were at odds, though unaware of why at the time. You were wrong, at that time, to try and take me by force. Your hand was raised against me in anger and mine against your men in return. Many of your soldiers died that day, for which I hope you will forgive me."

"But it not this matter I have come to discuss, but rather another. With me rides the King of Mulghazanzar and a company of his knights. Yet we bring no bounty of gifts or treasure, as the King beside me and his men can testify to. However, I have brought one thing of greater value than any treasure. This is your own foster son Avtandil, who rides with us. We await your invitation, for the road to Arabia has been long and difficult."

CHAPTER 51 –

THE MIGHT OF ARABIA

Rostevan looked at the messengers as though they had not finished speaking. Whatever words he might have uttered were caught in his throat. For a moment, it was as though he had been turned to stone and could no longer speak. But gradually, the color returned to his cheeks, and he came back to life.

He laughed loudly and joyfully, clapping his hands like a child. Tinatin, the shining sun beside him, grew brighter as though new light rays had been added to the countless brilliance she commanded. Her eyebrows and lashes cast new shadows across her cheeks of ruby, making more perfect that which had already been perfected.

The courtyard around them began to erupt with cheers and shouts of laughter at the news of Avtandil's return. Massive kettledrums began to beat rhythmically throughout the kingdom. Soldiers busied themselves, preparing to meet their leader and hero. Many were they who wished to run across the fields to meet Avtandil, but none would dare take that honor from Rostevan and Tinatin.

Instead, horses were prepared, and a carriage was made ready for Tinatin. Knights and men mounted around the King in such numbers it seemed an army was readying itself to march toward war. Across the gathered hosts, shouts and cheers could be heard. Many thanked God for the eternal triumph of good over evil as they went to the gates and erupted into the open road beyond.

The waiting heroes saw the distant flashes of sunlight reflected from armor and heard the horns and drums of men on the march. It was as though a wave of humanity broke against the desert sands and raced to them. Avtandil pointed as they came, hanging his head in shame as he opened his heart to Tariel.

"Look there and see what comes! The plains are dyed with the color of dust as the armies of my foster father approach. I am consumed with guilt for breaking his command and abandoning my duties. It is as though my betrayal returns to me again. Now I drown in a sea made from every tear any person in Arabia has shed over my absence."

"How can I tell you of this pain? No man alive has carried more shame than I now hold. But he is not here for me. It is you he comes to meet, and though he might wish to see me, I cannot appear before him like this. Whatever you intend to do must be done by you and Phridon alone. It is not within my power to attend this meeting or face the hosts of his eyes and their disappointment in me."

Tariel turned to his friend and put a hand on his shoulder. He waited for the Arabian to look up at him before answering.

"It is good you show such respect to Rostevan. Though he is your foster father, he is still your lord. Because of this, I agree with you. You should remain here. Phridon and I will meet the King. I will tell him why you have not come."

"Perhaps, through the grace of God, we will see you forgiven by your King for what you have done on my behalf. Then we can reunite you with your own sun Tinatin. Now, wait here. Let us find out what will come from this meeting between kings."

With those words, Tariel and Phridon mounted their horses and rode away to meet Rostevan and his armies. Avtandil remained behind with Nestan and Asmath. The two women believed Arabia would joyously welcome Avtandil home. But they were not at all sure how Tariel would be received.

After all, he bore responsibility for the deaths of Rostevan's men. This left them worried and fearful. What if the Kings disagreed and fought with one another again?

CHAPTER 52 –

THE BLOOD OF KINGS

Tariel and Phridon sat straight in their saddles as they rode to meet the hosts of Arabia. Neither was shy of themselves. They were kings and men of equal stature. How they might address one another was quite different from that of servant and master.

But the distance between them was no small matter. It was nearly half a day's ride in one direction. Because of this, the sun had passed mid-day before the two groups drew close enough to meet. As was customary, the kings would meet one another alone, with their soldiers remaining some distance behind.

First came Tariel, who dismounted and strode forward by himself. His figure rapidly closed the distance between them with bold strides. On the other side of the field, Rostevan came forward, an equally powerful king.

When the two met, Rostevan honored the King of the Indians and embraced him like a father to a son. Tariel returned the gesture, and the two men kissed the cheeks of one another. Rostevan wondered aloud how God had made such a mountain of a man, commenting on the breadth of Tariel's chest and the power of his arms.

"Now that I have seen you closely, I fear to lose sight of you. You are indeed a sun, and your absence would cause my day to become night. Truly, no more worthy king than you has ever stepped foot in these lands."

And then, as Rostevan finished speaking, Phridon also came forward. They met and greeted, each paying homage to the other. Yet the King of the Arabs looked past them, wondering where Avtandil was. He had not seen the youth, and his eyes turned towards Tariel with an unspoken question gazing out from them. But the Indian expected this and was quick with an answer.

"Oh, King, your presence has made a subject of my heart. Nearness to you has caused me to become a student of your worth. But how can you speak so well of me when Avtandil belongs to you? How could the sight of any other please you more than him?"

"And it is this which makes me ask more. For, do you not wonder where the youth is? Have you not considered why he might be keeping himself from our sight? But yes, from the look in your eyes, I can see you have thought this very thing just now."

"Let me assure you, he is well, though a malady of spirit plagues him. I would share the cause of his pain and explain why I could not bring him directly to you. But first, I must beg your forgiveness, for there is a favor I must ask of you. Let us sit, and I will explain."

Curious to know why Avtandil kept himself hidden, Rostevan called servants to make a tent for them to sit in. Sweet black teas and meats with various other Arabian delights were brought out. Interested in what Tariel would say, the King invited him and Phridon to sit and then took his seat.

Outside of where the three great kings sat, a vast host of Arabian men and women were singing. Others offered prayers to God, for they had not seen Avtandil yet. But a few brave souls pressed close to the tent in the hopes of hearing what was said. They were not disappointed.

Tariel broke the silence with a smile. His teeth shone like new pearls, lighting the room brighter than a lamp. With carefully chosen words, he began telling Rostevan why Avtandil had hidden away.

"Great King, I feel unworthy of mentioning these things to you, but it is the sum of my purposes here. You see, I have come before you in service to Avtandil. I beg you, on his behalf, to consider these words. For he is like a sun to me. His rays fall softly upon my heart, and I am forever indebted to the service he has rendered me."

"Because of this, I approach you equally from my desire to serve him. For it was this youth who sacrificed everything he loved to help me. You've undoubtedly heard some measure of how lost I was to the world, but you know only the tenth part of my story. Yet, I will not burden you with the retelling. We are all equally wearied and have no power for such a tale today."

"Instead, I will tell you of him. How he gave himself so fully to my cause that he forgot his own. What woe was mine alone too soon became his, equally afflicting him. Yet, I do not know how much of this you know."

"He did not abandon you without cause or reason. Nor did he flee his duties like a traitor. It was only through great pain and suffering that he could tear himself away from your side and his responsibilities to Arabia. And more, his departure was made with the blessing of your own daughter, Tinatin. Though you may not have known this, let me tell you, and you will understand."

"You see, I was once like Avtandil. I loved the daughter of my King but said nothing of it to him. Instead, our love was kept a secret. At least, until the day it was used against us."

"Much of what I cared was brought to ruin by our secret. How much I might salvage from the ashes of what we cherished of our home remains to be seen. I would not see this tragedy befall you or Avtandil, so I tell you plainly. Your children are in love with one another. Do not blind yourself to this or let them believe you do not see it."

"Tinatin loves Avtandil, and he loves her in equal measure. I have seen him tear-stricken and pitiable for want of seeing her. And in all these long years of service to me, he has gone without seeing her, who he desires more than life itself. So, I beg you, do not leave them to be consumed in the fires of love kept hidden."

"Let your daughter be wed to him. He has arms enough to protect these lands from invaders and a heart stronger than any I have ever known. I will ask no more from you than this, and in asking, bind myself to you."

With these words, Tariel stood up. He wrapped a cloth from his vest around his neck as though he were a student or a servant. Then he got down on his knees in front of Rostevan and placed his head on the ground before the King's feet.

CHAPTER 53 –

TO SERVE AND PROTECT

The King could not believe his eyes when Tariel bowed and made himself a servant before him. He knelt beside the Indian and pulled him up, speaking to him as he did so.

"Rise up, I beg of you. You are a king among kings. Do not reduce yourself to this position, or you will forever sadden my heart and deprive me of joy. How can it be that any man would not willingly give whatever you asked of him?"

"Truly, I say, even had you asked me to marry my daughter to a slave or send her to death, how might I have denied your wish? What man has the power to refuse you, and who but a madman would dare argue against your decision?"

"But you are a man of light, and your lips have not uttered darkness against my daughter or me. Rather, you have lit the sky with the beauty and truth of your words. We both know she can find no other man like Avtandil in all the universe, even if she found wings and flew to Heaven!"

"As for me, if I did not love Avtandil, why would I have longed so much for the return of his presence? He is a light and a sun to me, and I could not hope to find a better son-in-law than him. But you know this. I am certain you have seen it in him, or he would not have inspired you to speak as you have done on his behalf."

"Of the kingdom, there is nothing to give, for Tinatin has it all. She is regent, equal in all things to me, and more, the true ruler of Arabia. I am old, and the flower of my youth is spent, yet she is a new rose. Within her, life blooms anew. It is she who will carry our kingdom and our hearts."

"How can I object to this in any way? With God as my witness, I confirm these words and wishes as my own. Let the two of them be satisfied, and His will be done here on earth as it is in Heaven."

As the King spoke these last words, a murmur could be heard spreading through the crowds gathered outside the tent. Those who listened to what he said were astonished. They could not believe their own ears. Their whispers of a marriage between Avtandil and Tinatin spread across the crowd like wildfire.

Tariel, overcome with joy at the words of Rostevan, hugged the King, who held him close. Their faces glowed with happiness at what had been agreed. They were true kings who could embrace the truth and receive joy as their reward.

They knew honesty was its own reward. For whoever is honest lessens the burdens and lightens the hearts of those who walk the path of light. In this way, the will of God is realized through the hearts and minds of men and women equally. Smiling, they turned to the lord of Mulghazanzar, and asked if he would bring Avtandil.

Phridon, pleased to be the one who would invite the youth and bring the good news him, excused himself. He went from the tent and raced to fetch the youth, riding fast and hard. When he reached the place where Nestan, Asmath, and Avtandil waited, they ran out to hear what news he carried.

None could believe his story, but they knew it to be true. Still, Avtandil remained shamed. Though he rode back with Phridon, he kept his face hidden, even when entering the King's tent.

Rostevan saw him, hiding the light of his face behind a cloth. It was as though the sun hid behind a cloud, and a measure of darkness seemed to cloak Avtandil. But no matter how hard one tries to hide a rose from the light, it cannot be forever concealed. The ruby and rose of his cheeks would not long be hidden by shadows. Of this, the King was sure.

He had missed Avtandil and wanted to look at him. For years he had not seen the face of his foster son, and it pained him. Many a night, he worried himself to sleep. But the youth bowed, kissing Rostevan's feet and hugging his legs tightly. Frustrated, the King ordered him to rise.

"Stand, and do not be ashamed of yourself. You are loyal to me, but I never doubted this. So why should you carry shame in my presence? Your prowess has been revealed. The fires of worry consuming me have been quenched by the gentle rain of your return. But there is more."

"Tariel told me of your love for my daughter, whose eyelashes have shepherded your heart these many years. I know of your feelings for one another, and tomorrow I will join the two of you in marriage. You, oh lion, will be united with the sun you have longed to see. So do not hide yourself or your face, especially not from me."

When Rostevan finished speaking, Avtandil stood. For

the first time in nearly two years, they hugged one another Father and son, lost to the difficulties and trials of life, were at last reunited. Then the King bade the youth sit next to him, and they spoke at length of many things.

Sometimes Tariel or Phridon would join in, all of them sharing joy in equal measures at the reunion of the King and his foster son. But then Avtandil realized he had forgotten something. He turned to Rostevan and, with an apology, interrupted the King.

"My father, I cannot believe we sit here and speak of anything other than why you do not wish to see the sun. Just across the fields from where I came sits Nestan Daredjan. She is the flower of India and the bride of Tariel. The last princess, who married the last prince and saved the line of kings."

"For what reason do we delay? Let us go and meet her, so we might properly invite her into the palaces of Arabia. There she can meet Tinatin, and the two can rest and rejoice in the company of one another. Come, let us go to her!"

As one, the men realized they had indeed entirely forgotten Nestan. Each had been so worried about Avtandil, Rostevan, and Tinatin that they thought of nothing else. Then, when the tension was released, they allowed themselves to relax. Phridon laughed at the realization, jokingly teasing Tariel that he'd too soon forgotten his bride.

The four of them rode back to the tent where Nestan and Asmath waited, laughing and joking. Before long, they came close, and Nestan came out. The radiance of her presence dyed the cheeks of all four men the color of a setting sun. To see her and be near was to be healed of all pain and cured of all ills.

CHAPTER 54 –

A NEW MOON OVER FRESH SNOW

When they reached the tent where Nestan and Asmath waited, Rostevan dismounted, greeting the lady, and bowing. He felt blinded by the lightning flashing from her face as she kissed him first on one cheek and then on the other. When she stopped, Rostevan spoke.

"In all my days as King, there has been but one sun in Arabia. This is my daughter Tinatin. We see a pale and jealous imposter above us in the sky. But now, as I look upon you, I wonder with what words I might find sufficient means to offer praise."

"You are not a second sun but rather an equal. With two of you to light the heavens, how can there be bad weather or sorrow in my kingdom? If I were to look too long on your beauty, the roses of my gardens might wither from jealousy. I think only a madman would try to compare you to anything on this earth."

"But you must join us in the palace. There, you will meet my daughter Tinatin. She is to wed Avtandil tomorrow, but tonight we will celebrate our guests, the kings of India and Mulghazanzar. And as a special joy, my house will be graced with your presence."

"It has been too long since we held a celebration. I can think of no better reasons than your arrival and that of my daughter's marriage!"

With those words, the King clapped his hands, and they all made their way towards the palace. The three heroes accompanied him, and Asmath followed. But beyond comparison to any of them was Nestan. The sun seemed to follow wherever she went, but try as it might, in no way could it outshine the light of her beauty. Neither had it ever been able to compete with Tinatin.

At any other time, the sight of Avtandil returning would have been enough cause for the people to celebrate. Yet now, there were two heroes of equal measure riding beside him. Tariel rode to one side, his powerful form astride the midnight black steed he rode. Phridon was on the other side, long dark mustaches hanging down the sides of his beautiful face.

But more than the sum of these heroes was Nestan. Her brightness blinded those who looked at her as if they stared into the sun. But burned as they were, none could stop staring, for the sight of her brought comfort to the weary and soothed the hearts of the sorrowful. As they rode, more people came out to see this stranger who could only be compared to Tinatin.

In time they came to the palace, dismounting and entering the royal halls where Tinatin sat on her throne. She whose beauty caused woe in the hearts of those who saw her and left many souls lost to longing. A crown of pure gold was nested in her hair, and the scepter of rulership rested across her legs.

From the edges of her mouth, one could see the slightest hint of a smile. She knew who approached, despite never having met them before. First came Tariel, a hero of the old world and King of the Indians. Beside him stood Nestan, a mirror of the sun which Tinatin was. Yet their beauty did not compete. Instead, it was enhanced by their nearness, like two flames increasing the intensity of one another.

Phridon was next, the proud and dutiful knight and King of Mulghazanzar. Asmath stood with him, her dark hair covered with fine silks of blue and white. But most important to Tinatin and dearest to her heart was the man she loved. He who entered last.

Avtandil looked up as he walked to her, his smile beaming like a new moon over fresh snow. Here was her hero. The one who brought peace to her spirit and carried her heart in his chest. Just as she held his. Her lover had returned, and all the light and joy in her world was restored.

Tinatin stood and asked them to come forward. One by one, they came and paid homage to her, bowing and saluting as befitted her station. After this, she invited them to sit and began asking about their adventures. Each of them gave what answers were their own to provide. Some added bits and pieces to help with the telling as the tale of their shared adventures unfolded.

Their talk went on throughout the evening celebrations, and she listened intently. It seemed to any who came that the light of her face was brighter than anything they had seen. It was as though the sun and moon gathered their light together and shaped crystal and ruby into cheeks, with jet for eyelashes and stars as eyes.

The celebrations slowed when the hour grew late, and the heroes were shown to their chambers. Fresh fruits and Arabian delicacies were waiting for them, with sweet teas and fragrant wines. The finest silk robes had been laid out near their baths. And new clothes were also provided, with the old ones taken away to be cleaned by the house servants.

None of them wanted for anything that evening, save perhaps Avtandil and Tinatin. Of those two, they had not been able to speak alone. Yet their eyes said words only lovers could have heard. Those two fell asleep in their separate rooms. Dreams of the other danced through their minds until birdsong woke them to the morning sun.

CHAPTER 55 –

ROSTEVAN'S WISH

The guests refreshed themselves in the morning and changed into new clothes. Then Avtandil brought them to a private hall where they met Rostevan and Tinatin. They broke their fast together, enjoying fresh pastries and special treats made just for them.

When they finished, Rostevan invited them outside. To the amazement of Tinatin, there was a stage set with her throne. It was just like when her father crowned her as King Regent. But this time, his throne was also next to the one he had given her.

She turned to him, questions in her eyes. Yet he said nothing. Instead, he took her hands and sat her upon her throne. Once seated, she started to say something, but he silenced her with gentle words and a raised finger.

"There is nothing in the world more precious to a father than his daughter. For you, I have made this kingdom and brought order to our lands and those which border our frontiers. Yet there is another who will do more for you than I have. He will hold your hand as you mother your own children. This man will walk beside you through every step of life. It is with him you will grow into your old age."

"For all my years, I never knew who he would be. I was not certain from what lands such a man might come or if I would know him as your husband when we met. But now I have learned these things, and though I did know him, I was not aware he would be your husband. In truth, I think there was a time he also did not know it."

"However, my words grow long, and I will not delay the will of Heaven. The time has come for you to be united with the man who will be your husband. It is with my love and blessings that I present him to you."

Tinatin looked more confused now than before. She started to say something, but this time it was Tariel who interrupted her. He was a King like her, and she could no more deny his words than her father's.

"What transpires today is by decree of the Supreme Judge. Through your desire and wish, this thing has come to be. Yet, at this moment, your throne suits you more than any other before. For now, sun of suns, we seat the lion of lions beside you, in his rightful place."

To the amazement of Tinatin, Tariel and Rostevan took Avtandil by the hands. They seated him next to her on Rostevan's throne. This man, who she loved so much. Her heart raced at the sight of him.

And Avtandil, who traversed the entire world in her name alone, was now beside her. His heart was no less slain through separation than it was now by nearness to her. She was better to him than all things in the world. But sitting beside her now was more than he had ever dared to hope for.

For it was in her name alone that he had sacrificed everything. Not even the loves of Vis and Ramin could compare to what was shared between Avtandil and Tinatin. This was not something he only knew. It was a lesson he had lived and learned over the many years that had separated them.

For her part, she was at once shy and bashful. The love she felt for her hero had been a secret. She did know her father was aware of it, but she quickly understood it was Tariel who had told him. Still, she paled a bit at the suddenness of it all, her heart racing and hands shaking. Her dream came to life here, though not how she had expected it might have happened.

Rostevan looked tenderly at her as he saw her timidity take shape. He smiled as he lifted her delicate chin with his hands and looked into her eyes. Then he spoke to her and stood, addressing Avtandil as well.

"My child, do not be bashful of me. Everyone in this world finds love, though not all love what they find. The two of you are blessed by He on High. It is said by sages that love such as yours will never fail. For this reason and many others, I give you and your union my blessings. May it be the will of God for you to enjoy a thousand years of happiness."

"Let your days together be met with joy and in good health. Moreover, may Heaven see that you do not become fickle in your affection towards one another. Rather, remain steadfast like a rock. And for myself, may God grant me long years to see your love bear the fruit of children."

Then, the King raised his arms. Trumpets blared, and the heavy rhythmic thump of kettle drums began to sound. The ground shook as men and women marched into the square, which before had been empty. At this moment, the marriage of Avtandil and Tinatin would be made official by Rostevan, King of the Arabs.

CHAPTER 56 –

THE GLORY OF ARABIA

The King raised his arms high as the elite guard of his armies entered the square. At their head rode General Shermadin, childhood friend and confidant of Avtandil. The man could not help but smile at seeing his lifelong friend on the throne. He shared equally in the joy of Avtandil's happiness like a brother and a parent, only stopping to salute as Rostevan spoke again.

"You, soldiers and knights who are the backbone that supports the strength of our empire, look now to the thrones of Arabia! Before you sit not one King, but two, for on this day Avtandil has my throne, as is the will of God. Keep my commands intact and serve him in faith and fealty as you have served me these many years. Give him what he is due, and he will shelter and protect you as I have."

Then Rostevan lowered his arms, and all the soldiers on the fields and in the courtyards bowed down in servitude. Those men who couldn't be seen on the roads and hills beyond also bowed. The entirety of the kingdom gave fealty to Avtandil. For them, there could be no better outcome than to see the hero of Arabia marry Tinatin.

Of the soldiers and elite guard, Shermadin stood first. He turned and saluted the two kings, Avtandil and Tinatin. Then he spoke, and at each pause between his sentences, the soldiers hit their chests and shouted their assent in unison.

"We are forever sworn in service to you. Our lives are wed to the kingdom, and our spirits are woven into the fabric of the realm. It is you who magnifies and elevates those among us who are obedient. From your actions are the hearts and souls of our men encouraged."

"Through your wisdom are we able to see the weakness of our foes and cause their arms to fail. By your order, shall we return those disobedient back to the earth from whence they came. For you, and forever to the glory of Arabia!"

At the final words from Shermadin, the entire guard shouted a great cheer. It was louder than any heard in the kingdom before. All around them, men and women echoed the joy of the guards. Horns blew and were accompanied by the thunderous cacophony of kettledrums hammered in unison. As the sound died down, Tariel stood and spoke directly to Tinatin.

"In you rests the glory of hope, from which your empire was founded. Now you are united with the hero of Arabia. No longer will the flames of separation lick at the edges of your hearts. May your rule carry on throughout eternity."

"More, as your husband is my sworn brother, I also take you as my sister. Let none ever stand between you and him or what you shall decide in your kingdom's name. And to those who are false or opposed to you, I will bring them to ruin!"

Then Tariel turned to Avtandil, and he smiled. Brilliant white teeth shone from his glowing face. He laughed with joy as he spoke to the new King and husband.

"Brother, few knights are valorous enough to become kings, yet here you sit. The road of life has taken you from being an orphan to crowning you as the King of an empire. Your hands hold more now than I imagine you ever dreamed."

"But in all you've done, your heart remained forever faithful to those you love. May you always keep such a heart. It will forever be a light and a guide to those lost in the dark. I am proud to see you and your bride as kings of this land."

With those final words, Tariel bowed and stepped back from the thrones. Then a small procession of dignitaries and influential men and women of the kingdom came out to give their blessings. At last, only one old man was left of their number. This man was Sograt the Wise.

He winked at the crowd before turning and leaning down to give a whispered message to Avtandil and Tinatin. Although those closest could have heard what he said, they did not. The trumpets sounded as he spoke, and his words were lost to all but those they were meant for.

When the noise of the trumpets died, servants brought bread to sate the appetites of the gathered armies. Meanwhile, porters and palace staff members carried out tables and place settings. Silk cloths were placed, and ruby cups and golden plates were set next to bowls of jacinth.

Massive fires were lit in the pits to roast meat, while honey and cheese were brought out to further appease the hunger of the wedding guests. Soon, different colored vessels carrying wines of one type and then another were brought to the tables. As the drink began to flow, so did the conversations of those in attendance.

The faces of those there were awash with a blend of awe and joy. Their happiness was increased beyond measure at witnessing the union of the two people they loved most in the kingdom. Avtandil sat as lord and high King, made more beautiful by the presence of Tariel, who remained next to him. Phridon and Asmath sat on the other side from them, and between them rested something that amazed and dazzled all who saw it.

CHAPTER 57 –

WITH THE BLESSING OF GOD

This thing was the combined beauty of Tinatin and Nestan. Those who saw them together said they looked like twin suns. Their union made it seem as if Heaven had bent down to earth and spilled the glory of its joy into cups of the human form. Whoever came near could not stop themselves from bowing and paying homage to them both.

In truth, no small number of people there compared the gathering of those six with Rostevan as the seventh with the Seven Great Lights of Heaven. Though there was some discussion about who each light might be, in the end, it mattered not. Their faces all shone with rays of light, which cascaded over the guests in an endless stream of joy. Whoever was there and heard the words spoken or saw those heroes and maidens wished their heart to be in that place forever.

The celebration lasted three days, with Tariel acting as a groomsman for Avtandil. All the while, minstrels came and went, weaving through the crowd like shapeshifters. One minute a man on the harp, and next, a lady with a flute. Sometimes a duet, singing like nightingales, or an acrobat whirling like a dervish while clashing cymbals.

Around them were heaps and hills of gold, cut rubies, and emeralds. Food and drinks were delivered over and around these piles. Wine flowed like a fountain from hundreds of different spouts. Days went into nights which became morning and then turned into more days. The sounds of celebration never ceased or slowed their pace.

No matter their station in life or in the kingdom, each person who came received gifts. Everyone received something, from servants with pockets spilling out gold and silver coins to lords and ladies with fists full of precious stones. Pearls covered the ground, more numerous than the sand from which they were formed. Satin and gold cloth were everywhere and of less account than the silk napkins forgotten on the tops and edges of tables.

But as the morning of the fourth day dawned, Rostevan ordered a different celebration. The kingdom had come to see their new King for the previous three days. And all of them had been well cared for. They received gifts and love aplenty from their new rulers. But today, there would only be gifts for a select number of people. Specifically, the kings of India, Mulghazanzar, and the two ladies in their company.

Turning to Tariel and Phridon, Rostevan announced the change he was making. And as he spoke, he also ordered luxurious sofas and divans placed near him to accommodate his wishes.

"There has been no greater joy in my life than to gaze upon the beauty of Nestan and Tinatin. More, it is my great pleasure to know you, King of kings, and a comfort to see her as your bride. But how can I claim worth or wealth when you sit beneath me?"

"I am no more than the dust beneath your feet. Fit to have my ears pierced and set to work as your servant. It is wrong for us to occupy the same space. For this reason, I have brought couches. You and your queen will take your rightful place upon our thrones, and we beneath you at a lower station."

Phridon and Asmath moved to the middle couches at his words, and Avtandil and Tinatin sat on the lowest sofas. Then Rostevan took Tariel and Nestan by the hands, seating them on the royal thrones. After that, Rostevan began to behave like the host of a party.

He abandoned the dignity of royalty in favor of entertaining those he loved. To one, he brought a drink. And something to eat for another. Then he gave them gifts from his own hands. His generosity knew no bounds and was unmatched by anyone then or since.

Firstly, he presented Tariel and Nestan with gifts he piled in a heap. There were two scepters, with matching jeweled crowns in ermine and purple. Then, a thousand red gems, each the size of a Roman hen egg. This was followed by a thousand shimmering pearls the size of dove eggs. Finally, he gifted them a thousand war horses, each one the size of a small hill. Honestly, he treated them as his own son and daughter-in-law.

Next, he turned to Phridon, one well accustomed to his kingship, and Asmath, his guest. He gave them nine trays of black and white pearls, followed by nine richly saddled steeds. This was followed by more gifts and, in the end, a dowry for Asmath befitting a queen.

Rostevan continued to give them all gifts, some smaller and others larger until it seemed they might need their own army to carry such things home. In return for the honor of giving them the highest seats and the favor he showed them, Tariel bowed down on one knee. He gave the King of the Arabs a more respectful and dignified homage than any man would ever again receive from the King of the Indians.

For one month, the rulers played and sported together, enjoying wine and food until it seemed they might not need to eat or drink again. They continued giving gifts back and forth until rubies and jewels were treated like breadcrumbs in a bakery. All the while, the radiance of Nestan and Tinatin shone over them, lighting their faces and hearts with joy.

With sorrow, the day came when Tariel could delay his departure no more. He called Avtandil and Rostevan to him. Though it pained his heart to do so, he asked their permission to leave.

"To be near you is to rediscover the comfort and love of home again. I was so long removed from these things that I have forgotten all but the tenth part of them. Yet, they are returned to me in your house and through the grace of your hospitality."

"My joy is renewed, but I cannot sit here forever. The enemies of India hold parts of my kingdom, and I do not have news of Pharsidan or the Fate of our armies. My people need me, and they need Nestan. Our duty is to protect the people, for the knowledge and art of the learned are forever superior to the ignorant. Because of this, we must beg you to release us, or the kingdom of India may be forever lost."

"Surely a hurt to me will equally injure you, and I would not bring this pain upon any of us. Should we remain here much longer, I fear our selfishness might once more invite the evil of Fate upon us. However, with the blessing of God, we will not be long in returning to Arabia. Then we will celebrate the joy and grace of your hospitality once more."

CHAPTER 58 –

THE FOOLISHNESS OF FRIENDS

Rostevan looked at Tariel as he spoke, sorrow etching his face. Though he knew the truth of the Indian King's words, it was still painful to hear them uttered aloud. He wished his new friends could remain, but he could not delay the inevitable. So, he released them with a blessing and a final gift.

"Be not bashful before me. You alone know what is best for you in this matter. I cannot individually aid you, nor will I cause your road to become rocky by making promises I cannot keep. However, it is within my power to assist you. Let Avtandil accompany you and with him some part of the hosts of Arabia."

"With this help, you are certain to overcome every foe who stands against you. To those who have proven themselves traitorous, cut them to pieces and throw their corpses to the dogs. Let the crows feast on their eyes and innards and leave their ruined bodies as a warning to any who would dare to betray their oaths and vows."

Tariel showed a steely smile at the words of Rostevan. To be sure, he would do at least as much as the Arabian King suggested. Of this, there was no doubt. Blood would be shed, and no small amount of it.

Yet he did not want to take Avtandil away from his wife. They were just wed, and he had spent barely one month with his new bride. Turning a curious eye toward the young knight, Tariel asked his thoughts.

"Tell me, you who has finally grasped the sun and united yourself to her as husband and protector. What do you think of this? Are you ready to leave so soon? First, it was three years you spent in search of me. Then nearly another two years to find and rescue Nestan."

"In total, there is a debt of five years lost between you and your wife, for which I am the cause. Are you in such a hurry to leave her and roam the fields with me again? I think it is too early for the moon to leave the sun with which he has only just been united to. Is it not better for you to instead guard what you have won at so great a cost?"

Avtandil smiled as he listened to Tariel. He knew his friend well and understood the purpose of his speech. With a laugh, he answered.

"Do not attempt to seduce me with your honey-laced words. You know well it was Tinatin who sent me to find you. More, it was she who gave me her blessing to return and help further aid your cause. Do not think the sun of her spirit is so shy as to hide behind clouds when the time for war comes. She would have me no other way than as a man who keeps his vows and aids those in need."

"No, this is not the truth of your words. You do not want to leave without me, but it is you who are bashful and shy. You'll go away alone and take pity on yourself, claiming I left your side out of love for my wife. Woe to you who has been forsaken by friends in the hour of his need. Hah! I see the game you play at."

"Then I would sit here in Arabia. My sword would collect dust as I waited months and years for news from India. In time I would become pitiable. What sort of man do you ask me to be? Should my wife and I forsake our friends in the hour of their greatest need? Bah! It is a disgusting sort of people who would do such things!"

A smile spread across Tariel's face as he listened. It shone like the morning sun over an endless ocean. He leaned back and laughed, nodding his head in appreciation of Avtandil's quick and sharp wit.

"Ah, it is true. Without you by my side, I would surely bemoan the absence of my dearest friend. My every day would pass with an agonizingly slow tread. Each step forward would be more painful than the one before. I do not know how I would survive."

"But as you wish to come with me, how can I say no? Only, I beg you, do not accuse me of flattery in this. It is not me who compels you, but rather yourself. Who am I to stand in the way of an Arabian King?"

The two laughed at one another, knowing their path to India was decided. They would forever be committed to one another as friends and brothers. Phridon was no less committed than they, but he shook his head at the foolishness of his two friends. At least, he thought, one of the three needed to set the example of behaving like a king.

CHAPTER 59 –

A Bittersweet Affair

With their course decided, Avtandil called Shermadin to his side. This time, he would call on the service of his friend. They sat with Rostevan, Tariel, and Phridon, discussing battle plans. A map of India was laid out, with the borderlands and rival kingdoms outlined. There was no doubt the fortress Tariel called home was secure, as it was impregnable and manned by men loyal to India.

However, there were other areas and regions, not the least of which were those bordering the lands of Ramaz the treacherous. Meanwhile, Persia's uncountable armies would have been assaulting the eastern areas of India. Without their Amirbar, this would have left Pharsidan and his generals alone in the defense.

How much of the kingdom remained intact was unknown to Tariel, but they formed a battle plan. Rostevan would send eighty thousand Arabian knights to accompany the heroes to India. The companies of knights would be divided into four equal parts of twenty thousand men. Tariel, Phridon, Avtandil, and Shermadin would command one army each, working in unison to destroy their enemies.

The Arabs were no strangers to conflict with Persia and knew well their tactics and how to counter them. Because of this, there was no concern about managing that threat. As for the other kingdoms and armies they would face, they had yet to see the military might of Arabia.

With heroes leading the charge, none could stop their advance. Their victory over the soldiers and generals of their enemies was inevitable. But time was the one foe they could not easily overcome. They needed to prepare themselves and ride out with haste, lest the remaining defenders of India be overwhelmed.

Rostevan gave his own counsel as well and agreed with their war plans. But he carried an ache in his heart, knowing their departure would once more rob him of the sight of Avtandil. Though he understood it was necessary, it did not lessen his pain.

He was reminded of the first time Avtandil had left so many years ago. Tears came to his eyes with the memory, for he loved the youth no less today than then. But just as before, he said nothing. It was not the way of a man or a king to burden warriors with sorrow before a battle.

Meanwhile, the maidens held their own counsel, separate from the men. They were all equally lions, as Sograt had once told Rostevan, but to be equal does not necessarily mean to be the same. They were not students of the sword and had nothing to contribute to the battle plans. Though it would be their hands and sharp minds which rebuilt and ruled the kingdom when it was reclaimed.

But these were tasks that would consume much of their time. And they would not see one another for many years.

This made their parting bittersweet, for their love of one another had grown over the last month. Asmath, though not their equal, was still a friend and companion to them.

Yet Nestan and Tinatin were like twin suns. To compare them justly, one must be well acquainted with the movement of heavenly bodies. No different than the star of dawn when the moon rests level with it, they shone with equal brightness. If the light of one goes dim, then the other must also be extinguished.

But if their lights do not fade of their own design, then the sky will cause them to disappear with the turning of the earth. Then, one must make a hill or a mountain of themselves to catch even a glimpse more of their light. Otherwise, their brightness fades over the curve of the world. And for Asmath, she was a blanket of night sky which held and supported their glory.

They had sworn an oath of sisterhood to themselves, each trusting the words and promises of the other. To leave so soon seemed to them like pulling fruit from a tree before it was ready to fall. The twisting and tugging of their hearts hurt, though they knew it must be done. They hugged and held one another, chest to chest and neck to neck. Many were the tears of crystal that fell from their eyes.

Yet it was the will of He who created them which brought the two into the same house, and so it was He who would separate them. Though perhaps they did not see it through their sorrow, this was necessary. Despite the danger of war, Nestan needed to go with Tariel. Only together would the people of India support them and accept their rule.

But for the people in Arabia who witnessed their sorrow at parting, they were heart torn. The lights of those twin suns dimmed with the pain they endured. Those who saw counting the tragedies of their own lives as nothing in comparison.

Asmath looked at the two maidens, pity and sorrow clouding her rosy complexion. She had endured much hurt and loss over the years while she and Tariel searched for answers. Being no stranger to pain and suffering, she stood by to aid her friends as they consoled one another.

Parting was a bittersweet affair, but she was better acquainted with it than they were. However, to her surprise, Nestan turned to Tinatin and began speaking.

CHAPTER 60 –

PRISONER TO LOVE

Nestan opened her heart to Tinatin, speaking from the depths of her spirit. She called her new sister over and renewed her promises.

"You, who I had no knowledge of, have consumed me. I could not imagine another had the power to compel my heart so utterly, yet you have moved me as no other. Would that I never knew you, perhaps I might not suffer the pain of parting so intensely. Separated from the sun of my twin sister, I find myself melting for want of your light."

"Promise to tell me about yourself and the happenings here in Arabia. Send letters and gifts, and I will do the same. Truly, I am burned with want of nearness to you and know your suffering will be no less in my absence."

Tinatin took her hands in hers. Two delicate vessels of clay wed to one another in sympathy and adoration. She leaned her head close and let the majesty of her words bathe Nestan. She wove a cloak of eloquence for her, expressing the depth of affection mirrored to her sworn sister.

"But for the night, I had never known darkness until the moment I imagined myself deprived of your presence. Though a rainbow might fall from Heaven and a cascade of colors bathe me, I would see only gray without you to color my world. You are a delight to all who gaze upon you."

"I do not know how I can give up these moments that have illuminated my soul's most secret spaces. How will I endure separation from you? It is better to count my days as less for each not spent in your company. Truly, I pray to God, may you live for as many days as the tears I shall shed in your absence!"

Once more, they hugged, kissing one another like two small sisters. But they could not stay like this forever. The moment must end and only be kept in their hearts until they meet again.

They left, one looking back, longing for what she lost while the other watched as her heart drifted away towards foreign lands. Flames consumed them both, and only Asmath kept them whole, this one who was forever patient and kind. She promised to assist them in every way, and only through this promise could they finally separate from one another.

Apart from their sorrow, another brewed, though this one had been long in the making. Rostevan, for all his composure and experience as a king, wanted no more than to utterly forsake the lordship. He would have traded his kingdom to accompany those heroes, yet he could not. In their absence, there would be none other than him to assist Tinatin with the kingship of Arabia.

Avtandil and Shermadin would be gone. Should any difficulty arise, Sograt the wise and Rostevan would need to help guide and steer matters of politics. The forced impotency of the lordship and his age maddened him. He sighed more often than a husband waiting for news from a midwife about the health of his love and new child and cried out in woe at his plight.

But he could do nothing. Like a man fishing for sustenance in the sea, he was the subject of Fate. What would come would be, and his hands could do no more than bait the hook of hope before casting the lines of devotion into the sea. The catch he might bring up was not his to decide. Nor would the Fate of those heroes be in his hands. For this, he lamented but knew there was no power he held, or which existed on this earth to change what He on High had decreed must be.

Tariel, for all his cheer and bravado, was also unable to hide his sadness. Despite the jokes he made and the fun he took at Avtandil's expense, the truth of his sorrow was written on his face clear as day. The Arabian King had become something of a father to him. Separation from Rostevan burned his heart. The ash of those fires fell like snow across his face, graying his cheerful demeanor and wasting away his happiness.

As they left, Rostevan embraced each of them once more. First, the ladies Nestan and Asmath, followed by Phridon and Avtandil. In the end, he came to Tariel.

The power of his embrace crushed the rose of the Indian's form, but he did not deny the King. He let himself fall into the arms of Rostevan's fatherly love. It was a thing he had long since forgotten the meaning of and was only now reminded by as the King spoke. Hot tears tugged at the corners of Tariel's eyes, but he steeled himself and listened.

"Like a dream, you have come to me. And now, like the whisper of a morning yet to be understood, you go. My suffering will increase with each step you take from these lands, but I will have no succor from it. This heart of mine will be forever chained here, a prisoner to my love for you. For it is not just one of my sons who leaves this time, but now two."

"I did not know the meaning of life until it was shown to me by the valor of the men I am a father for. You have given me life, but I am slain without you to light my days. Do not be too long in your absence. Come soon, for I would rest my eyes on you once more before seeing the light of Heaven."

The kingdom's men stood ready behind them as he finished speaking. Then the heroes who would lead them mounted. Tariel was last to take the seat of his horse. He turned, desperate to stem the tears fighting to break forth from his eyes. Looking at Rostevan, he spoke briefly before riding into the sunset without looking back.

"My King, and my father, may these words forever grace your thoughts whenever your heart longs for me and finds I am absent. The sun forever hastens to greet you, as seen with each new dawn. Why should you not also rush to meet it?"

"In your sorrow, do not ask why you should hasten your steps to meet what you desire most. Let your heart be free, and find the truth of all you love in that freedom. I will find you in every sunrise and be waiting for you with each sunset."

CHAPTER 61 –

WHEN THE WORLD SHAKES

These were the last words anyone spoke as the armies of Arabia began their journey toward the distant lands of India. More could be told, and other things remain to be written. But there would be no reason here for the telling.

Of those who stayed and some who went forward, their eyes could not be removed from what was lost. They were utterly consumed, like grape vines in the fire. Not even the tenth part of their pain can be told with paper alone.

One might be inclined to say the road the heroes and their armies took was long, but it would not be accurate. For, between the lands of Arabia and India, there was no road in that time. What paths they took were trackless and desolate. None had been where countless men now made their way.

But the armies were well provisioned. An army of nearly equal size kept pace with them, made of porters and supply wagons. Among them, no small number of minstrels and bards had joined. Here and there, an acrobat or other performer could also be found.

And so, each night, there were performances and songs to carry the armies forward, and every morning a warm meal to keep strong the resolve of every soldier. Yet there is no point in telling stories of the roads they took to India. In the end, all paths are one if they lead to the same destination.

Man and horse alike wound forward in seemingly endless ranks. Each wore the finest Khwarazmian armor. Tariel's men had worn the same when they brought war to the Khatavians.

There was no better armor to be had in all the world. It was forged in the lands of Guldursun-Kala with secret knowledge Alexander had brought with him from Macedonia. The metal and weave were tempered in the Aral Sea's deep waters.

Between their armor, the Damascus steel of their blades, and their tireless steeds, the Arabian army was unstoppable. But the story of their march needs no telling. What should be heard is the tale of their efforts to liberate the prize of India and her Seven Kingdoms.

Armies of Persians sent by Khvarazmsha would have undoubtedly led the primary attacks on India. And without Tariel, the Amirbar and defender of the Seven Kingdoms, most border regions would have quickly fallen to the attackers. However, the palace of Pharsidan would have remained supported and defended by nearby the fortress Kingdom of Tariel.

His knights were well-versed in combat and equally proficient in city, field, and siege warfare tactics. However, other parts of the kingdom would undoubtedly have been overrun. Some by force of arms and others through betrayal or treachery. No doubt the hand of Ramaz would be seen at some point too, but those things did not matter now.

The first concern of the Arabian armies was reinforcing their troops with mixed units. To do this, they needed to quickly liberate as many parts of India as possible. This was because their army was entirely made up of mounted knights. Without foot soldiers, they would not be able to siege enemy fortifications. Nor could they hold and defend liberated territories without sacrificing the main advantage of their primary fighting force.

But Tariel had a straightforward and brutal plan. It relied on a series of carefully orchestrated strikes. After these precision attacks, his tactics would shift depending on the types of soldiers he was able to rally from the remaining forces of India. Following each new assault, he would adapt his strategy to account for new battlefield elements and the different types of reinforcements he hoped to muster.

His plan would succeed mainly because they would enter India's border with a larger army of mounted knights than the world had ever seen. This would dictate the initial tone of their assault, which relied on speed, precision, and overwhelming force. They would use this to their advantage, quickly moving past the outer edges of the Indian frontier and into the heart of the kingdom.

The main charge would be led by Tariel, with Avtandil and Phridon attacking the left and right positions to sow chaos in the ranks of their enemies. Shermadin would bring up the rear, protecting the supply lines and keeping Nestan and Asmath safe. However, once the initial charge broke the ranks of their foe, Shermadin would move forward with fresh soldiers to reinforce their positions.

Because they were attacking from outside of India, any defensive works they came across would be facing into the kingdom. This meant their attacks would be made from the rear, making fortifications easy to overwhelm. Then they would be burned and broken, leaving only smoldering ruins in the wake of their assault.

In this way, any reinforcements sent by the armies of Khvarazmsha or whoever else might have taken up arms against them would not benefit from abandoned fortifications. But, to say the plans of these heroes worked flawlessly would be a gross inaccuracy. Like all military engagements, neither horse nor weather behaved according to plan. There were setbacks, balanced by surprise victories and unexpected reinforcements.

Surprisingly, their most significant difficulty was not in reaching the palace but in liberating those kingdoms occupied by the Persians. The engineers of Khvarazmsha had built fearsome war machines which left many Arabians and Indians bereft of life and limb. Yet even the greatest defensive works of their enemy were eventually brought to ruin.

In total, it took almost three seasons to defeat the main elements of the Persian army. But the heroes were able to overcome their foes, for none could stand against their combined might. Anywhere they found traitors to the kingdom, those men and women were executed where there stood.

But some of their enemies escaped. Chief among them was Ramaz, the treacherous. He slithered back to his hole, but Tariel let those go who fled the battlefield. He would remember their names. And when the kingdom was secured, they would be reminded of his.

CHAPTER 62 -

LOYALTY AND DEVOTION

Across India, the citizens celebrated their liberty. The faithful sang the names of Tariel and Nestan in the streets beside those of Avtandil and Phridon. In the end, the heroes accomplished all they hoped for. The entirety of the Seven Kingdoms was liberated.

Those who were rightful rulers had their lordships restored. The traitorous and their kin watered the earth with their blood, and in their places, new rulers loyal to India were appointed to the vacant thrones. The joy of these victories caused Nestan and Tariel to forget their previous suffering.

Happiest of all were Pharsidan and his Queen. They had lost hope of ever seeing Nestan or Tariel alive again. Finding them both well and together gave them a joy that knew no equal. There were endless hugs and tears shared between them, and Pharsidan called for a huge celebration. One where he would officially pronounce Tariel and Nestan as the rightful King and Queen of India.

On that day, trumpets blew high and sharp notes over the palace grounds while cymbals sweetly clashed like quarreling nightingales. Copper kettle drums vibrated the earth and those who stood on it. Meanwhile, minstrels sang as acrobats danced and twisted, entertaining the old and young alike.

And what a joy it was to see the new King and Queen together. Their faces were lit with the radiance of two suns. It seemed like beams and rays of brightness shone across all who looked at them. It seemed as if nothing could cause them to shine more brightly until Pharsidan brought out the gold and jeweled key of the royal treasuries.

Those gathered could not hide their surprise at seeing the sacred key. Few ever saw it, save when a new King was crowned. For this key was a treasure. It opened the deepest and most mysterious vault in all of India. No one had laid eyes on what was in that vault for more than a thousand years. Only legends and whispered writings in dusty tomes hinted at what might lie within. But Pharsidan knew this, as did every Indian.

He ceremoniously placed the key in the center of a red velvet cushion with gold and emerald trim. Then he gave it to Tariel and Nestan. And with this key, the final piece of the ceremony was complete. The legacy of India was theirs now, as was the stewardship and protection of her people.

The citizens of India could not have been happier. Nestan was returned to them, and Tariel had taken his rightful place as King. People filled the streets, cheering and celebrating the return of their hero. But one thing that didn't sit well with the new King. Turning to Phridon and Avtandil, he raised an eyebrow before speaking.

"Brothers, do you not feel as I do that something is missing? It is as if there were an excess of space in my throne room. Yes, that is exactly the problem."

"We need more thrones! Else, where will my equals sit? How will the people properly show their adoration of you?"

With a laugh, he called the palace servants to him and ordered two thrones prepared for Avtandil and Phridon. Richly appointed and, of course, covered in gems and gold. These thrones were a testament to the valor and position of the heroes. More, they served a purpose.

When either of them was absent, those who came to call on Tariel would see the empty seats. Without needing to say a word, rulers and dignitaries alike would be reminded how the might of Arabia and the wisdom of Mulghazanzar were united with the power of India. None would dare challenge such an alliance.

Yet these were matters to be considered later by the wise men and advisors of the palace. It was time to celebrate now. Phridon, Avtandil, and Shermadin sat with Tariel and Nestan at their center. All around them, the people of the kingdom and many from afar came to visit. They joined together in celebrating the virtue and majesty of their King and Queen.

Every evening, the heroes recounted stories of their suffering and tales of the great battles they fought. Minstrels heard of years at sea and composed ballads of heroic deeds. Meanwhile, poets wrote verses recounting the beauty of Mulghazanzar. But chief among them were the traveling bards. They took the legends of battles against the Devi and the discovery of their countless treasures and retold them throughout the land.

As the days passed, great and small gifts were given to the people. Then they enriched merchants and travelers on their roads home. Of particular note was how the new King and his Queen took special care to ensure some of their wealth was also spread among the poor.

The common folk of India soon discovered their conditions were improved. Those who held the lowest stations were elevated, and their happiness shone brighter than those who had more and lived in better circumstances. But this was the most important lesson taught to Tariel and Nestan by their years of separation and suffering.

Those who are unacquainted with sorrow can find no pleasure in joy. Therefore, enriching those who have abundance will yield little results. But giving to those who have nothing will improve their lives and increase their loyalty to the kingdom.

This was a truth the new rulers saw time and time again. The lowest of their people were often the most loyal and joyous. They cheered their new King and Queen and praised Avtandil and Phridon in equal measures. Wherever they went, flowers and blessings rained down on them like falling cherry blossoms.

After a time, Tariel called Asmath to him. She, more than any other, was a hero to the people. She was not a queen nor any lady of the court. Instead, her role was that of a devoted and faithful servant. No one else compared to her in terms of sacrifice or loyalty.

The service of Shermadin to Avtandil or that of the two Knights Abu and Ardaz to Tariel were measures of loyalty and faith without comparison. There was no doubt of this, and in no way did anyone question it. But no one else woven into the tapestry of The Knight in the Panther Skin matched the loyalty and devotion of Asmath.

But because of this, her service was not easily rewarded. Those who ask for the least are almost always the ones who have done the most. Yet, a thing had come into the mind of the new King that no one in India had ever done. But he was not shy of breaking with tradition and said as much with what he awarded the maiden.

CHAPTER 63 –

THE LAST DAY

"Asmath, who gave life to the rose of our hearts when all we could see was winter. You who cared not for yourself or any want of your own, who had less than all others but still managed to give more than anyone. For your service to us, we give the only thanks we can imagine which can come close to rewarding your sacrifices."

"We pronounce you as ruler over the westernmost of our Seven Kingdoms. That which is closest to where we know your heart lies. From this day forward, you are royalty. Your sons and daughters will also be princes and princesses of India, for none are more deserving of this than you."

"For yourself, take whomever you wish as your husband. We will offer no argument against your choice. All we ask is for you and him to serve us with the same faith and devotion you have always shown to us and to India."

"Do not allow wealth and titles to diminish the richness of your character. You are a person who remains unmatched by any treasure in the world. Instead, give sweet to the sweet, and spend your days in happiness and joy."

Asmath was still for a moment, like a child who received a gift without understanding why. This was the beauty of her personality. She had never thought to receive anything, nor had she asked. Yet the gift she was given exceeded her ability to wrap her thoughts around.

She bowed low before her friend and King, kissing his feet and thanking him. But whatever words she said did not matter. All who knew her understood what a unique and beautiful character she possessed.

Wealth and power would not corrupt her more than sunlight and water spoil a rose. For her, receiving a kingdom was no different than receiving nothing. She would remain unchanged by wealth or lack thereof. Tariel had seen this in her before when they first met.

He had offered her gold and gems as a reward for her service in support of the love he and Nestan shared. But she refused. Instead, she chose a strange golden ring. And despite losing everything else, she had kept that ring until giving it to Phridon.

This gift to Asmath was made on the last day of the third season since the heroes left Arabia. Soothsayers would say one season had been gone for each of the three sworn brothers who had met. And each of them had aided the causes of one another three times. Perhaps what they said was true, but the words of sages are rarely noticed until long after they have been spoken.

Those heroes and friends were gathered in celebration. The foundation of their future had built on good omens and the blessings of Heaven. Each of them received gifts in such numbers and quantity that they soon counted pearls and jewels the way a child plays with sand at the seaside.

Horses were gifted in such numbers they seemed more numerous than blades of grass. And everyone was filled with mirth and joy. Yet the eyes of Avtandil held a secret. But unfortunately for him, his eyes forever betrayed the secrets they kept. Even if they had not, the lines on his face whispered stories of untold woe.

This was because he missed Tinatin. But not a word of his silent longing ever passed his lips. However, he did not need to speak of it. He was in the company of friends and sworn brothers. They were not blind to his suffering, and Tariel did not hesitate to address the matter.

"Despite the joy of our celebrations, I believe your heart bears an anger towards me. It seems I have kept you from your wife and have united your seven griefs into eight. However, I cannot forever keep you from your bride. Nor can you deprive her of the husband she has so long waited to be united to."

"Although I fear separation from you will allow Fate to begrudge me the joy I have found, this will be the last of our days together until we next meet. From tomorrow you must go. But first, let Nestan and I give you what we have decided suits our parting. Because my pity at your absence would not be a fitting gift for Tinatin."

Then, Tariel called to his servants, and they brought out gifts for Rostevan. Each was as unique and wonderful as the friendship they had discovered together. One part consisted of small and intricately carved little ships and cities made of gemstones and jade from the farthest eastern reaches of Asia.

Other items were from far and distant lands or remote islands. But then there were some gifts which were particularly unique. These were wrapped in silk, and to be kept secret until Rostevan opened them.

For Tinatin, Nestan brought out a shimmering cloth that seemed to have been woven from light. When she unfolded it, Avtandil could see it was a cloak and veil. But what it was made from, he knew, but Nestan did him a message for Tinatin.

"Take this with you, and gift it to my sister. You know already of the veils and cloak which Tariel gave me. But these were found in the treasuries of Kadjeti. I have never worn them, for the one my husband gave me is dearest to my heart."

"But these veils I give you shine like at night like a full moon. Wherever she goes with these, the light she is a part of will follow. And I will forever feel my hand is on her, and she is closer to me for it."

This and some small, jeweled pins were the gifts she gave Avtandil to bring back to Arabia. A single tear fell from her eye as she handed them to him. It splashed onto the edge of the veils as he took them, but Nestan smiled. Despite the sorrow she felt at the absence of her sister Tinatin, she knew they would not be long or far apart. This gave her comfort and lifted her spirits.

Avtandil was full of gifts now, and though Shermadin and the armies of Arabia would return with him, the road would be lonely. He did not want to imagine how long his days might be without the company of his friends. But then Phridon spoke up.

CHAPTER 64 -

A Dream In the Night

"It pains me to add salt to the wound of Avtandil's departure, but I must also go. My own people await the return of their King. Doubtless, they will be burning to know stories of our exploits. More than this, no small number of traders in my kingdom will be eager to make a road towards India with every type of goods."

"I've much to manage, but so do the two of you. You still need to settle enough into the lordship to realize what burden some parts of it can be. But my feet will often tread the halls of these courts, for I desire your company much like a deer desires the cool waters of a mountain spring."

With those words, the course of the heroes was decided. Two of them would leave in the morning with Asmath. Her journey would take her to the westernmost of the Seven Kingdoms, which was not far from Phridon's home of Mulghazanzar. Tariel and Nestan would stay, which was their duty as the King and Queen of India.

The next day Avtandil, Phridon, and Asmath mounted

their horses and rode off to the west when the sun cut its path through the morning sky. All around them, throngs of Indians wept as they and the armies of Arabia rode away. Newfound friends are rare enough in the world, but those whose hearts are true are rarer still.

Sorrow tinged the edges of their goodbyes, but they took joy in knowing the nearness of one another. And although the fires of separation would burn them long after they made their farewells, their spirits remained high. It wasn't until the time came for Phridon and Asmath to go their own way that Avtandil made a complaint.

He compared the bitterness of separation to the skin of a grape, forever cloaking the sweetness and joy of life. But his words were short, and their parting was a bittersweet affair. Though the time between their next meetings felt as though it would be long, in truth, it was not.

It was only the pain of separation which made the days seem to stretch into months. Consoling himself with this knowledge, he took his men toward their home in Arabia when their paths separated. What other time they spent on the road is of no real account.

The days were not much different than the ones before or after. One foot followed another. Some days it rained, while others were sunny and bright. The only constant aside from their path to home was the conversation Shermadin and Avtandil shared as they rode.

The young knight learned what had transpired in Arabia all the years he had been gone. He began to understand how deeply his absence had wounded Rostevan and the unspoken burdens Tinatin had carried without complaint. His respect and admiration for those he loved grew with each new thing he learned from Shermadin. So did his devotion to them and their causes.

He came to understand many truths in the words his

friend shared with him. Things he knew of but had not experienced began to coalesce into more firm ideas. Some he had been taught by others, like the wise and leaned Sograt. Yet there were things he had learned on his own. Chief among those was the person he became after his first three years alone on the road. It is easy to claim faithfulness when standing next to the sun. But it is another matter entirely to keep that faith when embraced by the night.

These thoughts and others danced through his head as he neared his home. Before long, the hero and his faithful servant saw the frontier fortress in the distance. A cheer went up from the men, and horns sounded from the far walls. They were nearly home, and the men who remained behind to defend Arabia had seen their approach.

Fires were lit along the walls. It seemed all the soldiers in the kingdom were there to greet Avtandil as he rode into the realm and made his way toward the Rostevan and Tinatin. There were endless cheers and shouts of joy for him in every city he passed until he finally reached the palace. There, he saw his sun and knew his troubles had not been in vain.

He sat with her on the throne. Together they beautified the realm. Those who saw them rejoiced, and he shared in their joy. The pain of his longing slowly left, and the light of Heaven shone on his union with Tinatin. He on High forever blessed the might and power of their rule, and they often celebrated with Rostevan.

As the years passed, the three sworn brothers met and celebrated often. All they desired and planned had turned out well in the end. Phridon found himself a bride, which is a tale for another day. Meanwhile, each of them found their kingdoms enlarged. Their might was increased, and any who disputed their rulership were put to the sword.

Those who lived in their kingdoms knew a golden age

as no other realm in history has enjoyed. The poor did not beg, and orphans found homes with widows, all of whom were enriched. So absolute was the power of their rule that even goats could roam freely without fear of wolves.

As for those who wanted to do evil, they fled the lands in terror. There was no place in the three realms where one who wished ill on another could find a foothold. None dared question the right of the three kings or their rule, and for a time, the world became a better place.

But all tales end like a dream in the night. Each of those heroes passed from the world the living and into the next. For this is the treachery of time, that however great a thing is, it must inevitably fall. Those who count any earthly kingdom as long are mistaken.

Those who count any earthly kingdom as long are mistaken. For it is us, the people of this earth, who exist for but a moment. No matter how big of a monument or mountain someone has ever built, the people who created them have all been forgotten.

But sometimes, a thing is so great it is never truly forgotten. A person can define generations, lasting forever as they become a part of what it means to be human. Sometimes, being human means being a hero

The legend of The Knight in the Panther Skin is one such story. Like dust from a falling star, the better parts of these tales mingle with the world around us and become part of who we are.

TO CLIMB A MOUNTAIN –

A LEGEND SPEAKS

Slowly, I came back to the reality of my surroundings. The story melted away from my eyes like a fog. It seemed to me I'd watched those great men and women march through their lives and down the long corridors of memory. In the space of my thoughts, I came to have a more intimate understanding of history and, in turn, the dust it all eventually becomes.

The winds of time forever blow the past across the world, where its ashes take root in the earth. It becomes a part of the water we drink and grows in our food until each of us carries it within. Every breath we take becomes a part of that history, and our steps echo those of our ancestors.

I thought of the places I'd been and those I had yet to be, but nowhere could I think of one which compared to the story I now knew. The guides I met on my journey were pillars of humanity. They belonged to a place too few people had seen and a time almost everyone had forgotten.

Noticing this was to become aware of a fragile thing, too easily overwhelmed by the hospitality and culture of the country. Although this understanding surprised me, its existence was now apparent in everything I saw.

I realized the people who came here were mainly like me. They were on a trip to enjoy themselves and see something foreign. Some few others were politicians and diplomats, here to push their agendas or make strategic agreements. But everyone who visited brought something new to a thing they didn't understand. This arrogance was unintentional, but in the end, not enough understood what they looked on. They only saw the places and the things which made it Georgia without knowing what the country really was.

This was invariably what happened to the people who came and left. Their visit to the cradle of hospitality did not disappoint. Nor did the sights of their Paris of the Caucasus. They made reservations or signed treaties without ever seeing Sakartvelo. Because of this, each of them left more than they took. They saw the outside of the book without really understanding the insides.

But no good book anywhere ever had a cover better than the insides, and countries don't ask to be understood any more than books ask to be read. And for the most part, no one invited me or any other tourist here. Even if they had, it's a bad guest who doesn't try to understand his host. But almost every visitor misses the depth of those they meet only briefly. In this way, some invariably saw Georgia as a restaurant or hotel, but only because they viewed it through the lens of their modern world.

Sakartvelo, on the other hand, was not any of those things. It was a home from which the cradle of Europe was rocked, and some of the world's greatest warriors were born and died. When one accounted for the history of here, every hill became a mountain. But I hadn't realized these things until Shota Rustaveli opened my eyes to them.

Looking out the window of the old but surprisingly comfortable GAZ M-20, I still saw the same country all around me. But I realized now how little I understood before and how much I still had to learn. For his part, the driver had already taken me to several places. One was outside the city of Batumi. That place, he said while smiling, was called Kadjeti by some, and Petra by others. And another, he told me, was the fortress of Gonio.

We stopped at many places, but when I asked where we were heading, he kept telling me I would see. Before long, we were surrounded by mountains and racing along a wide river. I thought to ask the name of it, but then realized I'd completely forgotten to ask the driver's name. Belatedly remembering my manners, I apologized and asked who he was. His answer, though informative, was anything but direct.

"Who I am doesn't matter. The only thing special about me is that I'm from Sakartvelo. Otherwise, I'm anyone you might meet or have met in my country at any time throughout history. We're all unique, and in that regard, we're all the same, which brings me a little closer to the end of our time together."

"You see, the story you've heard is complete. Save a few moments, which you'll discover soon. But before we make that stop, you must know a bit of what most foreign historians won't tell you. Depending on how you read the past, it may or may not have happened in Italy."

"No doubt you know how the renaissance is believed to have taken root in the hearts and minds of Italians before spreading to the rest of Europe. But there's a whisper of more to the story? Because this happened hundreds of years after the heroes of The Knight in the Panther Skin passed into history. By then, their names were forgotten by all but us."

"However, legend has it a man named Shota Rustaveli once carried the seeds of this story far and wide. Some say he even carried the tale to Italy before the renaissance. However, our history doesn't speak of this, even if world events might hint at it."

I wanted to ask more of him, but at that moment, he turned off the paved road we'd been on. Without slowing down, he went up an old track only fit for logging trucks, old cars, and men from other times. All I could do was hold on and pray we didn't run down the side of a mountain.

THE FORGOTTEN STORY –

SHOTA'S SECRET

When our car finally came to a stop, I was ready to kiss the earth. But looking from the windows, I was surprised to see we'd arrived on a mountaintop. I'd heard of Georgian high mountain settlements, but this was the first time I was visiting one.

Houses were tucked into or on top of the hills around us. Meanwhile, people of all ages crowded around the car, welcoming the driver and me as if we were family. Children ran back and forth, gleefully shouting and chasing one another as they ran between cows and dogs.

I assumed he knew them, but he just laughed, saying men like him were welcome in every home. But as for the people, he had no idea who they were. They were simply people of his country, which was all that mattered. He wanted me to see authentic Georgian hospitality before taking me to the last stop on my tour.

That evening we all sat together, sharing white wine

made from black grapes and small glasses of a honey infused local drink called cha-cha. All sorts of new food dishes were brought out which I'd never seen before. So much so that the tables overflowed with salads, meats, cheeses, and everything else someone could eat. Whenever I asked for the name of something, I learned a new word. And then the men and women began to sing.

The driver told me they were singing Adjarian folk songs. Music of the mountains, as he called it, from a group called Mokvare. People of different ages would sing in different tones. Sometimes with no musical instruments and others with things I'd never seen before. One young girl played a three-stringed guitar called a panduri. A young boy had a set of wooden Pan pipes called a larchemi. But most surprising was the old man playing a gudastviri, which looked and sounded for all the world like bagpipes.

Whatever they played always involved people singing in various harmonies, which was hauntingly beautiful. I wish I could say I remembered what they sang, but the words were all foreign to me. However, that night the spirit of those songs became a part of me, as did the high mountains of Georgia. There truly is no other place in the world like it. Nor, as my head can attest to, are there roads like the ones you'll take back down the mountain the following day after an evening of wine, cha-cha, and song.

To my surprise, the driver congratulated my performance the evening before. In particular, he told me I had carried my wine and the respect of the tables at which I sat like a real Georgian. This was kind of him to say. But I told him I'd woken up like an American. My head was not yet a qvevri, and my constitution was far removed from that of the mountain folk.

He laughed loudly at my comments and told me not to worry as we would soon reach our destination. True to his word, it was not long before we arrived at a place named Akhaltsikhe. It was an old fortress that had been restored, with towering walls and breathtaking views of the surrounding lands. To this day, it remains one of the most amazing things I've seen in the country.

As we walked through the buildings and halls, he told me to take note of the differences between the country people saw and the one I'd accidentally discovered. Then he reminded me of the answers I came seeking. He sat me down near a small alcove with an Orthodox Idol. it was there he spoke to me for the last time, finishing one story and beginning another.

"At any time and place in these lands, you will forever stand in two worlds. One of those places is known to everyone as Georgia. But the name true to our people's hearts is Sakartvelo. It is this place the author of The Knight in the Panther Skin comes from, and only there where you will find the other answers you seek."

"The end of his story, like all endings, is simply another beginning. However, only some from beyond our lands have attempted to understand what it means or where it might lead them. Listen well, for what I relate to you now is the ending Shota wrote. There are secrets in these words, and more than just his footsteps echo therein."

"'I who tell the story of The Knight in the Panther Skin am no more or less than a Meskhian bard from the land of Rustavi. These words have been composed in honor of King Tamar, served by David the sun. Yet you who may hear this tale should know it remains untold in any form other than verse.'"

"'For, it was through the elegance of poetry I strove to entertain she who knows no equal. Her whose majesty strengthens those who are loyal and utterly consumes the traitorous, striking terror in foes from East to West. But it should not simply be recited. Rather, let it be sung with the voice of truth.'"

"'Yet, you might ask, how will I softly sing these precious and rare tales of old from the harp of David? I tell you, loud will my song be of these strange and foreign monarchs. My praises of their customs and deeds will be sung and give praise to He on High for what they have done.'"

"'For this world is not to be trusted. It is too fickle and fleeting for the eyes of ordinary men and women to truly grasp. Here for a moment and gone in the blink of an eye. Yet here you are, those few who seek. So, ask yourselves what you want? But have a caution. Think carefully before you answer, for Fate will insult the desires of your heart and soul.'"

"'But for those few who find themselves favored by fortune, live well. Embrace happiness in this world and carry your joy into the next. For what light you make will be a guide to the less fortunate. And it is they who will sing these songs of old.'"

"'This is how Moses of Khoni gave undying praise to Amiran, the son of Daredjan. With him, praise was rightly sung for King Tamar and from the lips of the wise man of Athens, as told in Abdul-Mesia from Ioane Shavtheli. And let us not forget Sargis of Tmogveli, who sang the praise of Visramani and was most loyal.'"

"'Yet among them all, there was but one who sang the legend of Tariel in praise to King Tamar. It was this man whose tears never dried. This poet and bard whom in the end, none but the earth held.'"

His words flooded me with new names and information, none of which I'd heard before. As so often seemed to be the case with things in Georgia, the answers I found left me with more questions than I started with. In chasing the story of The Knight in the Panther Skin, I came to understand Shota Rustaveli in a way few people did. But now I had my arms full of new tales written by people who were Shota's contemporaries and maybe even his friends.

I had no idea what I might find between the pages of these other legends. Nor had I processed what I'd learned so far. But I was sure the old driver would tell me more. As with everything else, I had but to ask. However, when I looked for him, he was gone. Night had fallen, and in his place was an old, faded book with a handwritten note illuminated by the moonlight.

"Remember, not all rivers draw their water from the same source. Sometimes a person must be lost to find their way, and one could spend a lifetime looking for answers in Georgia. It would not be a wasted life. When you're ready to learn more, look for answers brought to life by the hand and brush of a villager like me."

"Find the mountain one man looked up to from warm waters while he retraced the path of another who lost his mind, both from under the same full moon. When you get there, stop to smell the flowers. Remember what it means to be a son and a brother to the animals of this earth. Until then, may these words be a guide to the next part of your journey."

Reading his note, I smiled. How well he knew me in so short a time, and how little I knew myself, despite so many years on the road. But I was not the same man I'd been when starting this adventure. Nor was I free to leave like the tourist I once was. I couldn't. Georgia had captured my heart.

საქართველოს გაუმარჯოს!
Sakartvelos Gaumarjos!
May Georgia Be Victorious!

THANK YOU!

We hope you enjoyed A Rule of Three.
Make sure to read all three books in the series.

Avtandil's Quest
The Road to Gulansharo
A Rule of Three

If you'd like to learn more about us,
please visit our website or follow us online!

https://hjbuell.com

@HJBUELL

ABOUT THE AUTHORS

H. J. BUELL

Henry is a native of Virginia who grew up between the majesty of the Blue Ridge Mountains and the secret societies of Washington, D. C. Over time his profession drew him into the wars of Afghanistan, Iraq, and the complexities of geopolitics. But one day, he left the war.

From there he traveled the old world on foot, staying in different countries, while learning their beliefs, cultures, and customs until reaching Georgia. While working as a lecturer and writer, a publisher introduced him to Shota Rustaveli's epic poem, The Knight in the Panther Skin.

The story captured his imagination, and he began working to translate the poem's esoteric, philosophical, and spiritual elements into English. However, it took seven years to accurately rewrite the epic.

And now, the complete series can be read in English for the first time in history. These books are Avtandil's Quest, The Road to Gulansharo, and A Rule of Three, and they are available in eBook and print, either online or from select bookstores.

ABOUT THE AUTHORS

ANA GABUNIA

A native of the old Georgian city of Kutaisi, Ana lived through the darkest times of modern Georgia. As a child, she studied French by candlelight and dreamt of making the world a better place. It was there, on her father's lap by the flickering light of a single flame, where she first discovered The Knight in the Panther Skin. He read the legend to her, and this ancient tale imprinted itself on her heart forever.

In time she grew from a little girl into a woman full of hopes and dreams. She studied diplomacy and journalism, working with the United Nations, where she tirelessly championed the rights of internationally displaced people, women, and children. Before long she worked her way into the Georgian Diplomatic reserves.

Eventually she traveled across Europe, yet the truths she hoped to find abroad weren't there. Instead, they were back home in Kutaisi, where her love for the beauty and philosophy of The Knight in the Panther Skin first blossomed. Realizing how few people knew the story outside of Georgia, she committed herself to bringing this epic tale to the world.